S0-AVJ-468

The Oregon Trail™

Copyright © 2019 HMH IP Company Unlimited Company. THE OREGON TRAIL and associated logos and design are trademarks of HMH IP Company Unlimited Company.

All rights reserved. For information about permission to reproduce selections from this book, write to trade.permissions@hmhco.com or to Permissions, Houghton Mifflin Harcourt Publishing Company, 3 Park Avenue, 19th Floor, New York, New York 10016.

hmhbooks.com

The text was set in Garamond.
The display text was set in Pixel-Western, Press Start 2P, and Slim Thin Pixelettes.
Illustrations by Gustavo Viselner

The Library of Congress Cataloging-in-Publication data is on file.
ISBN: 978-0-358-04058-3 paper over board
ISBN: 978-0-358-04057-6 paperback

Printed in the United States of America
DOC 10 9 8 7 6 5 4 3 2 1
4500766609

Wiley, Jesse,
Gold rush! /
[2019]
33305248950317
sa   10/20/20

The Oregon Trail™

GOLD RUSH!

by
JESSE WILEY

Houghton Mifflin Harcourt
BOSTON   NEW YORK

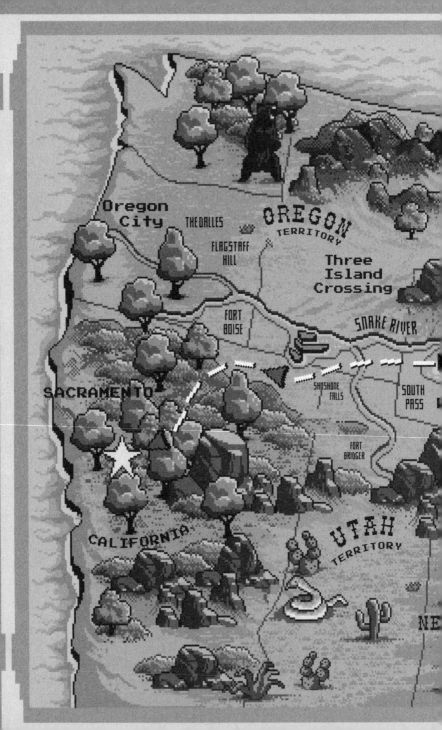

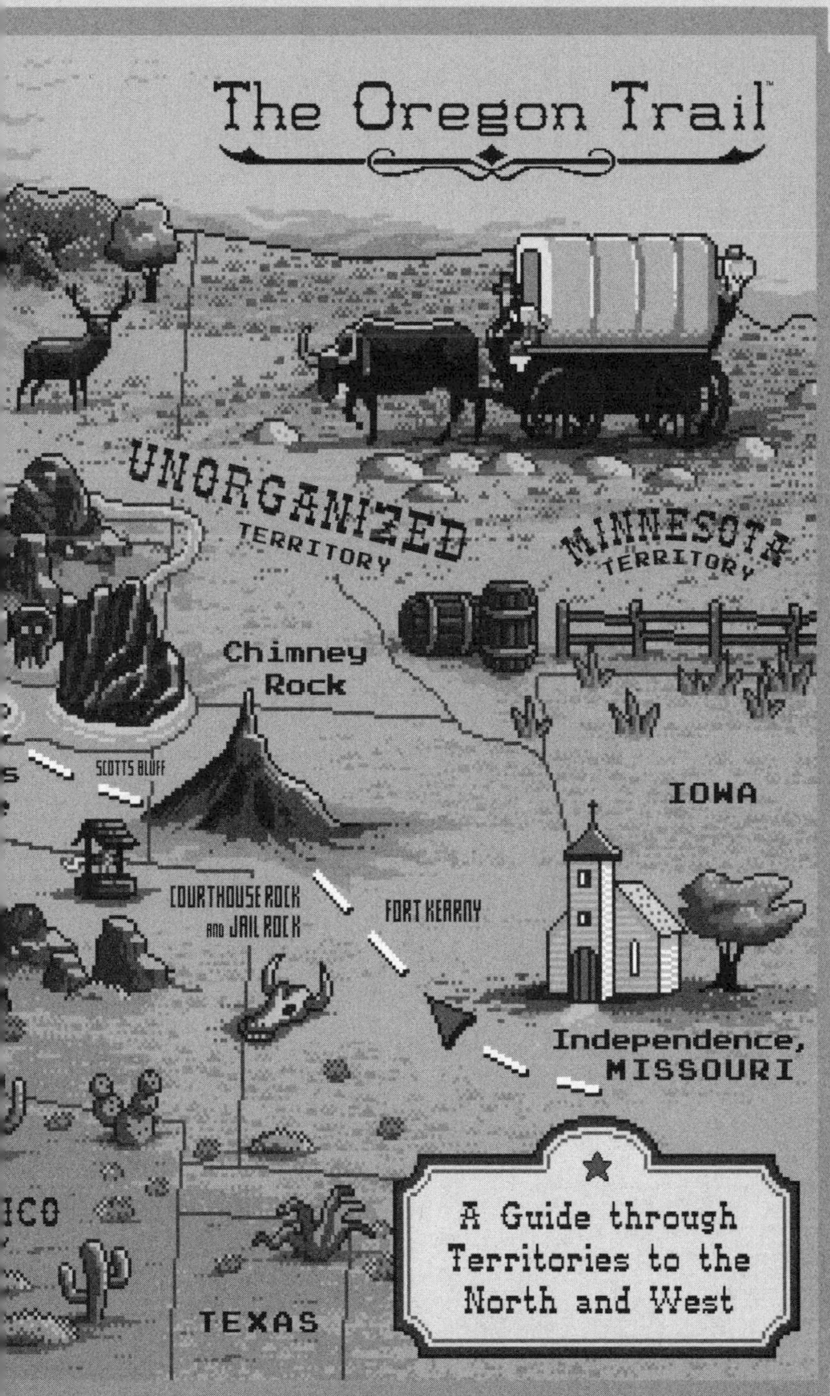

The Oregon Trail™
UNORGANIZED
TERRITORY
MINNESOTA
TERRITORY
Chimney
Rock
SCOTTS BLUFF
IOWA
COURTHOUSE ROCK
AND JAIL ROCK
FORT KEARNY
Independence,
MISSOURI
TEXAS
A Guide through
Territories to the
North and West

The Oregon Trail

Westward Ho,
Young Pioneer!

It's 1851. You and your family are on the journey of a lifetime: traveling roughly two thousand miles from Independence, Missouri, on the Oregon–California Trail. Along with thousands of other pioneers, you're headed west, hoping to strike it rich in the middle of the Gold Rush.

But your gold fever and excitement will only get you so far. There are many obstacles ahead, and you have to depend on your wagon train to survive. Often there will be no one else around for miles. Make sure to pack enough food, water, and supplies for your long trek.

It won't be easy. The Trail will wind through some of the most difficult terrain, including the vast desert. Remember to think creatively, rely on those you trust, and be prepared. You'll face dangers such as dehydration, sickness, ruthless bandits, starvation, and flash floods. Persevere, pioneer! It will take all of your skills and smarts to get to your final destination.

There are twenty-two possible endings full of obstacles, twists and turns, and incredible discoveries, but only one path will get you across the country safely. Will you choose to go to California or Oregon?

You're stranded in the desert—what do you do?

You're caught in a hailstorm—where do you find shelter?

Look out! Buffalo stampede! How do you escape?

Before you start, be sure to read the Guide to the Trail on page 158. It will help you make better decisions in the midst of calamity.

At some points on the Trail, you might run into other travelers, Indigenous nations such as the Potawatomi, or trail guides who can provide advice, assistance, and friendship. At other times, you'll have to trust yourself to make the right choices.

It's up to you!
What will you choose?

➡ Ready? ⬅

LET'S BLAZE A TRAIL IN THE

GOLD RUSH!

Lone Elm Campground
MAY 26, 1851

It's a cool evening in late May. Goose bumps cover your skin, so you reach into your covered wagon for a coat. The sun has just set in the Lone Elm Campground. Around you, the other thirty-nine wagons in your train rest close by. You hear laughter and music and smell the mouthwatering scent of meat and sweet fruit pies.

You let out a yelp when your little brother accidentally drops a tin plate right on your foot.

You groan. "Benji, you have to be careful."

"Sorry," four-year-old Benji mumbles. Your dog, Tippet, sits beside him, wagging his tail.

It's not really Benji's fault. He's only hungry—and so are you. "It's fine, Mukki." You 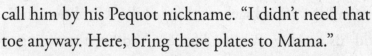 call him by his Pequot nickname. "I didn't need that toe anyway. Here, bring these plates to Mama."

Mama is pulling supplies out of the back of your covered wagon, getting ready to cook a hearty dinner. You run over to help her. It's been a long day.

You've been traveling for about twelve miles on the Trail to reach Lone Elm Campground from Independence, Missouri. You can't wait to sink into your bedroll.

"Just in time." Mama kisses you on the forehead. "Could you do me a favor?"

"Sure, Mama."

She nods over to a covered wagon some yards away in the corral. "Invite Mr. Southworth to join us, will you? We have plenty to share."

Although Mr. Southworth has been in your wagon train since the start of your journey, you're still shy. You've seen Mr. Southworth fix many bent iron rims, including one for your own family's wagon wheel. But you don't really know him that well beyond his great blacksmithing skills. Until now, he and his mother, Pauline Hunter, had been traveling, enslaved by the man you know to be their master. Half of your original wagon train—forty wagons out of eighty—split off a few miles back. The others wanted to take a northern route. Mr. Southworth stayed with your wagons while their master went north with Mrs. Hunter.

"All right, Mama." You start off to Mr. Southworth's wagon. "I'll be right back."

When you arrive at Mr. Southworth's site, he's preparing his own dinner.

"Hello, Mr. Southworth." You fidget and wipe your hands on your clothes, then relax as you smell the sweet aroma of baked apples in the air. "My mama asked if you want to join us for dinner. Though what you're cooking smells tasty!"

Louis Southworth is in his early twenties. He has a kind smile framed by a thick black beard. A pocket watch hangs on the vest of his gray woolen suit. "That's quite kind of you. I'll bring some food to share and be right on over."

You nod and skip back to tell Mama.

Mr. Southworth arrives and Papa and Benji are preparing supper alongside Mama. Mama cooks a juicy chicken over a spit while you and Papa peel potatoes. Benji runs around the camp with Tippet.

"Mr. Southworth! Glad you could join us." Papa rises to meet him.

"Thank you, Ben. I brought an apple pie to share. My mother's recipe." Mr. Southworth sets down the pie and shakes Papa's hand firmly. In his other hand, he holds an oblong wooden case.

"I hope your family likes apple pie, Kutomá." Mr. Southworth smiles at Mama.

You cook up a delicious meal of roast chicken, potatoes, cornbread with dried corn from your garden back in Connecticut, and fresh milk from Mr. Southworth's cow, Dilly. You wish you had a cow. Instead, you have three goats, two fat sheep, and a stubborn horse named Spot to herd them.

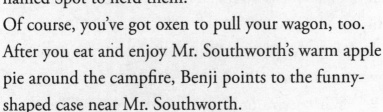

Of course, you've got oxen to pull your wagon, too. After you eat and enjoy Mr. Southworth's warm apple pie around the campfire, Benji points to the funny-shaped case near Mr. Southworth.

"What's that?" Benji's eyes widen.

"Come and have a look for yourself." Mr. Southworth flips open two silver buckles.

You gently pry the case open. "A violin?"

Mr. Southworth laughs and picks it up. "I'd call it a fiddle, but 'violin' works too. Would you like to hear it sing?" When you and your brother nod in excitement, he fits the fiddle underneath his chin and plucks the strings to test the sound. Pleasant twangy music echoes through the campground.

"Excuse me," calls a new voice. All of you turn to see Fergus McAllister, another neighbor, approaching. He looks worried. His shock of red hair sticks up on all ends, and his thick red brows are furrowed. "Sorry to interrupt." He has a thick Scottish brogue. "But I just hoped to have a word with you folk."

"What seems to be the trouble, Fergus?" Papa's brow furrows.

Fergus rubs his beard. "Well, I've been talkin' to a few other families and they're packing up and heading out. They heard from a local passerby that there's been a nasty pack of bandits called the River Rush Gang lurking about the Trail . . . and they're headed this way."

Papa and Mama exchange worried looks with Mr. Southworth.

"Will we be robbed?" Benji jumps to his feet.

Mama hushes him and holds him tightly to her chest.

You cup your hand to Papa's ear. "Maybe we should talk to Captain Beauregard. Tell him we should leave. Now."

"Hmm. I think we should," says Papa, troubled.

You go with him, Fergus, and Mr. Southworth to find the captain of your wagon train, John Beauregard, sitting at his own campsite with his wife, Stella, and their son George, who made a mean face at you earlier. You stay behind Papa, just in case.

"Excuse me, John." Papa steps into the campsite. "We need to talk." He tells John and Stella about the potential danger nearby.

"What are you suggesting?" John puts his hands on his hips. "We just camped down for the night. We can't up and leave *now*."

He's right: everyone is exhausted after the long day. The last thing you want to think about is walking more. But after hearing about the bandits approaching, you don't want to be robbed, either. You'd have nothing left for the journey to either California or Oregon—whichever you choose. And yet if you keep going now, your tired animals won't make it very far. What should you do?

To convince the others to leave now, turn to page **126**

To stay at Lone Elm Campground, turn to page **124**

You take the risk and follow the fur trappers. After all, this is the first real encounter with the Gold Rush that you've had. You don't want to pass it up.

"We should check it out, Papa." You nudge Papa with your elbow. "If it turns out to be nothing, then we won't lose anything, right?"

Papa nods, uncertain. You follow them out of Fort Laramie for a few miles until you reach a thicket of trees hiding a small rocky patch. You fidget a lot and scratch your head. You're so far from Fort Laramie, but this wouldn't be a *secret* gold mine if it were close to the bustling fort.

"It's over here." The leader of the fur trappers points to a circular rocky nook.

"And what is the reason you're sharing this with us?" Papa puts his hands on his hips.

The fur trapper grins. Two of his teeth are gold-capped. "Oh, we ain't." He whips out his gun from his holster. "All right, everyone. Empty those pockets of yers. The only gold up here is what you're handing over."

You can't believe you got duped. Now you have no money for the rest of your journey. You'll have to stay at Fort Laramie until you can earn enough to keep going on the Trail.

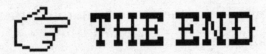 **THE END**

You can't wait and pass up this chance to bring
down a buffalo and source food to feed your family.
This is the first herd you've seen in the plains. As
Nikan said, buffalo are scarce—and who knows when
you will see more.

The buffalo might
be frightened and rush
off over the hills or . . .
trample you and Benji. You
ignore that potential danger.
You'd really love to eat something other than pilot
bread and bacon.

You gently push Benji behind you. "Stay close,
Mukki. And get ready to run if this goes bad." You
point your pistol at the nearest buffalo and pause.
You shoot; only the buffalo doesn't go down like you
expected. Its hide is too tough, and your pistol too
small. It stumbles off. But now, you've startled the
herd.

Oh, no. You shoot again, but you miss and waste
several bullets. The buffalo herd breaks into a full run,

circling around you and Benji. You're relieved as the dust settles. But then you look up and see that they're headed right toward your wagon train!

You run with Benji at your heels and scream to warn them. But it's too late. The buffalo crash into wagons, knock over livestock, and destroy supplies. They pass on, but the damage has been done. Luckily no one's been seriously injured or killed, but everyone is furious and looks to your family—to you, specifically—to blame. Some of them, especially the Beauregards, want you to pay for the damages. Some say that they want your family to leave. You know it's your fault, but you were only trying to help. All the same, should you separate from the wagon train to appease them, or try to apologize and stay?

To split up the wagon train, turn to page **44**

To try to stay together, turn to page **136**

Papa is depending on you to herd the livestock. Your feet feel sore, but you have a job to do, just like everyone else in the wagon train. Despite Mama's warnings to avoid riding Spot until after the storm, you are determined to ride your horse. You can herd the livestock *and* save your tired feet.

Every time you try to get close, Spot lashes out with a vicious kick. When you try to put the bridle in his mouth, he tosses his head and snorts in your face. "C'mon, Spotty."

Despite the approaching storm, the sun peeks through the clouds briefly, beaming down warm in the sticky spring air. You sigh and wipe sweat from your forehead.

"Look out!" Mama waves frantically.

But it's too late. The last thing you remember is an enormous hoof coming right at you. You tumble to the ground and black out. Your journey on the Oregon–California Trail is over.

 **THE END**

Mr. Southworth goes on with the rest of the wagon train. He doesn't want to fall behind. You'll need his help, but Papa is a carpenter and can do most of the work himself. Though it'll take much longer.

"I don't like leaving you folks behind." Mr. Southworth's warm smile turns to a frown. "But I do need to reach my mother in Oregon. The sooner the better."

Papa shakes Mr. Southworth's hand. "I know. Thank you all the same. I'm sure we'll catch up in no time."

Mr. Southworth waves back at you and disappears into the distance with the rest of the wagon train. You feel a deep pit forming in your stomach. Your family is entirely alone out here in the wild. Now you have no support of any kind. Danger surrounds you.

You try to help Papa replace the wheel, but you

really need Mr. Southworth's skills to repair the axle. Papa can't fix it himself. You're stuck until another wagon train comes along. But there's no guarantee that will happen.

You're so tired and hungry. You don't want to waste food rations, so you and Papa go into the hills to hunt jackrabbits. It's getting dark. You watch for prairie dog holes so you don't fall in and twist your ankle. As you follow behind Papa, you step on something.

Crunch! Hiss!

You freeze. A shape unwinds in the dark.

Snake! You've just stepped on its discarded skin.

Should you run or call for your father?

To call for your father, turn to page **65**

To run for it, turn to page **53**

You bypass the stranded wagon train. You want to help them, but you need to reach the Barlow Gate before winter arrives. Stopping will delay your trip significantly.

Your wagon train will notify someone at the next trading post or settlement about the stranded party. You go around the Gate of Death and continue along Snake River, passing Register Rock. You stop to carve your names into the rock alongside those of thousands of other pioneers.

That night, you wake to the sound of shouts and gunfire. Bandits ride into your wagon corral. They've

surrounded you and take everything you have. You turn back to Fort Hall and find a way to earn money there to save up for another trip to Oregon City next year.

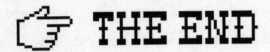 **THE END**

You help the stranded pioneers get back to Fort Hall. With Fort Boise, the last major fort on the Oregon Trail before desert and Blue Mountains, miles away, there aren't enough supplies for everyone.

The rest of your wagon train goes on without you, your family, and Mr. Southworth. With the wounded pioneers in your wagons, you start the long, slow trek back to Fort Hall.

When you reach Fort Hall, you're all so weary and don't want to turn back to catch up with the rest of your wagon train. Mr. Southworth goes on without you, but for now, you and your family will stay in Fort Hall to rest and find work. You decide to try for the California Trail next year.

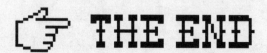 **THE END**

The land is already in the middle of a drought. Going through *more* desert won't help your situation much.

Then it clicks. You remember where you've heard the name Lansford Hastings before. "Mama, I don't think the Hastings Cutoff is a cutoff at all."

Her eyebrows arch. "How do you mean?"

"I read about it in a guidebook before we left. Hastings thought he was taking a shortcut, but it turned out to be twice as long a route as the California Trail. People died. I don't think taking the Hastings Cutoff is a good idea, Mama."

Mama's eyes widen. "You're right. I heard

something about that too. They got stranded in the mountains. Some cutoff that is!"

Papa agrees too. When you relay the news to your wagon train, you see uneasiness cast over many faces.

"Agree. Not a good idea." Fergus scratches his red beard. "We oughta go with the Kellers' advice, eh, Cap'n?"

"There has been a drought so far. Perhaps going through a longer desert road isn't the wisest decision this year." John Beauregard puts his hand on his chin. "We'll continue on to Fort Hall and take the California Trail from there."

The majority of people in the wagon train are relieved to avoid more miles of desert. From Fort Hall, your family can decide if you want to go with the wagon train to California—or go northwest to Oregon City.

You start off for Fort Hall in the morning. Over
the next two weeks, you make your way through
mountainous terrain. You stop at Fort Bridger, a
trading post, where you stock
up on flour and sugar. You
continue northwest and pass
through valleys surrounded
by low brown-hued
mountains. Then you stop for a day in Soda Springs,
an area of naturally bubbling waters.

"Caused by ancient volcanic activity." Harry
looks up briefly from a book on anatomy. "Some use
it as a cure-all." He nods to where everyone in your
wagon train is relaxing in the bubbling waters. "But I
wouldn't drink it if I were you. Even if it is naturally
carbonated."

"I wasn't going to." Your tongue is dry and sticks
to the roof of your mouth.

You finally reach Fort Hall, check your wagon for
any needed repairs, and rest. You see pioneers, U.S.
soldiers, and people from the Shoshone and Bannock
Nations come in and out of the trading post. You and

your parents run into Mr. Southworth in the fort's general store.

"I'm glad we're meeting here." Mr. Southworth shakes Papa's hand. "Thought I might miss getting a chance to say farewell in case we part ways."

"You're not going to California with the rest of the wagon train?" You stick your hands into your back pockets.

Mr. Southworth shakes his head. "No, afraid not. I've got to get to my mother in Oregon. But if you end up out that way, maybe I'll come down to visit, once I earn enough for the freedom of my mother and I."

"If we do go to Sacramento, we'd love to have to you both come visit." Papa smiles.

Your mouth already feels dry. "Can we go to Oregon, Papa? Isn't there gold mining there too?"

"Yes." Mama nods. "But we have family near Sacramento."

"It's good to be near family," Mr. Southworth says. "Fare thee well, dear friends. It's been a pleasure traveling with you." He picks up his goods from the counter, waves, and heads back to his wagon. You'll miss Mr. Southworth and wish you were going with him.

"What about the drought?" You turn to your parents. "Shouldn't we avoid the desert?"

"It's not something I've been looking forward to, I'll admit." Papa looks at Mama. "What do you think?"

Mama clasps her hands together. "I'd wanted to be closer to family, but . . . it wouldn't make any sense if we can't even get to them. But we knew this journey would be a risk either way, Ben. Oregon has its own dangers: snowstorms, avalanches, steep gorges. If we end up in Oregon, it'll be difficult for us to travel down to California later, and I think you know that."

"I know. Which is why I'm leaving the decision up to you." He hugs Mama. "This is about your family. If you want to go to California, we'll go. If not, I'm sure we'll make our way in Oregon too. There's gold mining there, and plenty of carpentry opportunities."

Conflict rages in Mama's eyes. She takes your hand. "What do you think we should do?"

What Trail should you choose?

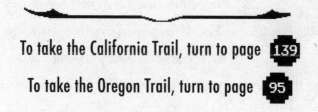

To take the California Trail, turn to page **139**

To take the Oregon Trail, turn to page **95**

Your stomach is unsettled, but the sharp pangs of hunger overtake your nausea. Some bread or johnnycakes might help. You throw johnnycakes onto the griddle beside thick slabs of bacon. Mr. Southworth and Papa are roasting a deer over the spit. You feel overwhelmed by the scents. You drink some coffee, but the bitterness makes you gag.

Still, when supper is ready, you wolf down the food. By the time you take a bite of venison, any appetite you had is now gone. Your stomach gurgles, but not from hunger.

"You all right?" Mr. Southworth frowns. "You look a little green around the gills, there."

"I'm fine." You hold on to your stomach.

"Just hungry? Here." Mr. Southworth takes a piece of cornbread and puts it on your plate. You can hardly bear to look at it.

"Thank you." You don't want to be rude and leave

it sitting on your plate, but you can't imagine taking another bite of anything.

You crawl into your tent, shivering and dizzy. You're up for the rest of the night. Chills turn into full-body shakes; you can't get warm no matter how hard you try. Dysentery ends your trek on the Trail.

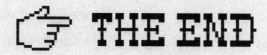 **THE END**

You continue along on the Carson Route. After all, you've only just met this man Jim Beckwourth—and you don't want to have to cross more desert without a constant water source.

"Thank you, Mr. Beckwourth." Papa nods. "But after everything we've been through, we want to make sure we stay on the route we've planned."

Jim Beckwourth tips his hat. "Can't say I'm not disappointed, but you folks take care. It's still a long and rough road to Sacramento."

You hope you've made the right decision.

You move southwest along the Carson River through the Carson Valley, cross over sandy terrain, and pass over rocky bluffs and ridges. You move away from the river to avoid traveling on a very narrow cliff. About a mile away, your wagon train passes a strange alkaline bed as clear as glass.

"That's not something you see every day." Mama squints. "It may look interesting, but don't drink it. It will make you sick."

You're relieved when you finally see the Carson River again, but the ground is still barren and dusty. Will you ever see green again? After miles of desert landscape, you see low-rising snow-capped mountains in the distance. As you travel, the brush becomes thick dry grass underneath your feet.

Eagle Station is the last stop before you cross into the Sierra Nevada. It's a trading post with travelers

from Mexico, traders from the local Washoe Nation, and pioneers alike. You and the McAllister children make fast friends with several Washoe children whose parents are trading with pioneers. One of the pioneer families even has two giant Newfoundland dogs, both of whom bark and run around with an excited Tippet. You almost don't want to leave.

Mama talks to a Washoe family and learns that the gold fever in Sacramento has already hit its peak; the land is overflowing with hopeful gold-seekers. Exhausted and not wanting to risk crossing the

mountains, your family decides to set up a small business there in Eagle Station. You fix passing pioneers' wagons and mine for gold in the Sierra nearby when you can. It's not Sacramento, but it's good enough.

 **THE END**

Apologies won't make things right. Even if you try to repay them for the damage, your family will be broke for the remainder of the trip and resentment will linger in the wagon train. The only way is to continue on your own without the support of a large wagon train.

"I'm sorry it's come to this." John wipes dust off of his brow. "But I appreciate your willingness to do what's right. You caused a lot of damage to a lot of property, and folks might not forgive you for a long time. Best leave to avoid any hard feelings from here on out."

Your parents nod sadly. Guilt overwhelms you.

Later that day, you watch the rest of the wagon train roll off into the prairielands without you. Your parents won't even look at you, much less talk to you for the rest of the night. A heavy silence looms over the campfire.

★ ★ ★

Your family continues on through the prairie the next morning. It's eerily quiet, like the calm before the storm. A prairie dog scurries away from your wagon and ducks down into a hole.

Then you see it: a great billowing cloud coming right at you.

"Dust storm!" Papa waves wildly. "Everyone in the wagon!"

You all get inside the wagon and draw the canvas down. Papa stays outside to keep driving the frightened oxen. The storm lingers for several hours. Boulders crash in the distance. When the sand and dust finally settle, you have no idea where you are.

Should you keep going to find Fort Laramie, or turn back to Independence to find a new wagon train?

To turn back, turn to page **105**

To keep going, turn to page **107**

Losing sight of the river isn't the wisest choice, what with the drought.

"What if we wait a day and cross the river?" You kick a rock away. "We've got a water supply. If the river settles down, it'll be easier to cross, and we won't have to go around it."

People like this idea. Even John Beauregard agrees with you. Mama and Papa smile down at you, proud.

"Maybe you should be the wagon train captain," Fiona pokes you.

You grin back.

Using buckets of tar, you and Papa caulk the wagon, filling the cracks between wood beams to make the vessel waterproof. While your family rides in the wagon, you use Spot to herd the livestock through the river canyon.

The river is narrow. Your wagon train starts off through Carlin Canyon, crossing the river slowly to get to a patch of land on the other side. You have to dig your heels into Spot's sides to get him to go into

the water, but with a few soothing words, he trots right through.

Your wagon train fords the river with no injuries and only a few valuables lost in the water. You continue along the Humboldt River, where the countryside grows drier and sandier by the hour. Dry winds sweep up and cause your lips to crack. You stop at a sulfur spring and pull out a map. You move your finger to where you are. The Forty-Mile Desert. This is where you part ways with the Humboldt River.

Your wagon train gathers as much water as they can carry and starts off across the endless sandy desert. Finally it becomes so unbearably hot and dry that your mother suggests you travel by night rather than day to avoid your animals becoming overheated. John agrees, and you couldn't be more relieved.

ay after day, your water rations grow smaller and smaller. You think this stretch of desert will never end.

One morning you see a man on a horse coming toward your wagon train. You hear a warning bugle sound, and the guards hurry to surround the wagon corral. The man on the horse waves his hat, calling out a friendly-sounding "Hello there!"

You go out with Papa and the others to greet him.

The man tilts the brim of his hat. He's got a friendly smile and wears the trappings of a trail guide

or possible fur trader. "Morning, folks. I'm Jim Beckwourth. I assume you are heading to Sacramento?"

"We are." John Beauregard steps out of the crowd stiffly. "Are you a trail guide? If so, I'm afraid we don't need your services, but thank you."

Mr. Beckwourth smiles. "When you hear what I've got to say, you might think differently, mister. See, I know the route you're planning on taking, and I'm going to let you in on a little secret: There's a better and easier way than the Carson Route."

"Is that so?" John shifts his weight from one leg to the other.

Mr. Beckwourth nods. "That's right. It's an old path that takes you on a gentler, lower incline route off the Truckee Route. You won't ruin your nice wagon wheels on the nasty Sierra Nevada going my way."

"And where does this 'alternative route' take us?"

"Gets you to Marysville, but it's a quick jaunt down to Sacramento from there." Mr. Beckwourth smiles. "Plus, there's a nasty gang of bandits going after unsuspecting pioneers all along the Trail, looking for gold nuggets and such. I've heard they're headed this way."

Your ears perk up. "The River Rush Gang?"

Beckwourth nods. "Afraid so, kid. They've been hunting for people carrying gold all the way from Sacramento to Independence, Missouri. Wouldn't want to get caught in their crosshairs."

People in the wagon murmur among themselves.

Papa raises his hand. "Maybe we should talk this over, John. I have to be honest: I like the sound of this cutoff. If what he's saying is true, then going at a lower incline could save our wagons a lot of damage. We know this upcoming stretch of terrain isn't going to be easy."

"Maybe so, but what if it's another Hastings Cutoff?" John looks at the crowd. "We can't risk it."

"You were willing to risk it for the Hastings Cutoff." Mama steps in.

John is speechless. "Well . . . you can risk it then." He stomps off.

Your parents turn to discuss the options with you. Beckwourth's route sounds much more appealing after days and days in the desert. What route should you take?

To take the Beckwourth Trail, turn to page **118**

To stay on the Carson Route, turn to page **40**

Papa's pretty far ahead, with Tippet bounding at his heels. By the time you call him, it might be too late. You bite your lip and watch as the snake unwinds even further.

The rattling grows louder.

You make a run for it. The venomous snake lashes out as you move. Pain shoots up your leg. You scream out for help, the roar of agony rushing through your ears.

This is where your journey on the Oregon–California Trail ends.

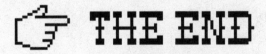 **THE END**

You take the Greenhorn Cutoff. The strong river current could carry away your livestock. You don't want to risk it. Plus, you'd have to cross the Humboldt at least four times to get through Carlin Canyon.

You start off west over the hills. It will be roughly eight miles on the cutoff before you rejoin the California Trail near Humboldt River, but until then, all you see are rolling dry hills and scrub brush.

As you continue on, a haze of dark clouds covers the once sunny sky. You're grateful for the respite from the hot sun—until the skies open up with heavy rain and booming thunder.

"Monsoon!" Papa is already drenched. "We need to be careful about flooding from the river."

The ground beneath you becomes thick, soggy

mud. Spot's hooves sink in deep, and all the oxen struggle to pull the heavy wagons.

You hear a crack—your wagon tips to one side. You see one of the wheels snap in two. Papa hurries to fix it, but the others don't want to wait for you in this bad weather. Should you split up and plan to meet ahead at the river junction? Or convince the wagon train to stay with you?

To split up, turn to page 94

To stay together, turn to page 113

You don't want to cause trouble, so you say nothing. Everyone is suffering and desperate out here in the desert. If you're not careful, a small argument could quickly become something much bigger. George is hardly older than you; you may not like him, but you know how hard it's been. Even if he is the thief . . .

The next morning, you discover that one wagon has disappeared. And much to your dismay, so has the rest of your water supply. The Beauregards stole it!

You're stunned. "The Beauregards . . . just left?"

"With our water supply." Papa puts his head in his hands. "They knew they'd gotten us lost out here in the salt flats. We never should've listened to them."

"But what are we going to do now?" Your palms sweat.

Papa shakes his head. "I don't know."

"I knew this Hastings Cutoff was a mistake." Mama's face screws up. "We never should have come this way."

There's nothing you can do. You're stuck in the salt flats, lost.

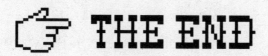 **THE END**

You help the stranded wagon train. If you were ones stuck in the Gate of Death, you'd need someone to be there for you. But when you, Papa, and Mr. Southworth try to get the other people in the wagon train to assist, no one offers.

"I'll lend ye me horse, Keller." Fergus pulls on his red beard. "But I cannot go. Not when ye hear tales about the River Rush Gang lurking about these parts."

Mr. Southworth points into the distance. "Those people need our help, Fergus."

Fergus shakes his head. "Wish I could help ye, Mr. Southworth, I do. But I won't risk it. Me family needs me."

Only you, Papa, and Mr. Southworth ride off to aid the stranded wagon train. You're not sure what you can do with only three people, but you have to try.

When you finally reach the narrow chasm of the Gate of Death, the situation is worse than you thought. The people have just been robbed by

the River Rush Gang, and others have been badly
wounded by rockslides caused by rain. They are a
small five-wagon train, but each wagon is damaged,
from broken axles to rotted wooden beams to missing
wheels. Supplies and food are strewn everywhere,
including a dead horse that makes you shudder just
to look at it. You could carry the wounded, but it
will be a slow walk back to the wagon train. There are
small children, and babies, even. Between your horse
and Mr. Southworth's, you can only carry a couple
people.

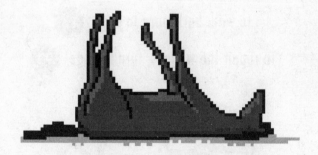

Mr. Southworth turns toward you and Papa.
"Should we try to fix the wagons? They look like
they're in a bad way. Might be too much, but we
could try."

Papa wipes his hands on his pants. "It might take too long—and the wounded won't make it if they don't get medical help as soon as possible."

"But we can't carry the wounded on our horses." Mr. Southworth puts his hand on his side. "That will be even worse for them. They'll need to be carried by two people, or laid on a wagon."

Should you try to repair the damaged wagons or help everyone to walk back to your own wagon train?

To walk back, turn to page **73**

To repair the wagons, turn to page **98**

You take a little more medicine. You've only had a few sips so far; maybe more will help. You tip the bottle back. Instead of a sip, you accidentally dump the rest of the bottle into your mouth. Coughing, your eyes fill with stinging tears. It tastes horrendous. Now your stomach feels almost worse than it did before.

You head back toward your tent and you still don't feel better. Your stomach rumbles and gurgles. You can still taste the medicine on your tongue.

"Where were you?" Fiona peeks out of her tent.

You jump. "Nowhere."

Fiona eyes you. "You don't look good. What did you eat? Drink water that's not boiled?"

"No," you lie. "I just . . . it's a bit hot tonight, isn't it?" You tug at your collar.

Fiona touches your forehead. "You really don't look well."

"Who doesn't?" Mr. Southworth walks by, holding his fiddle case.

"No one." Fever overtakes you and fire dances before your eyes. You waver on unsteady legs and then collapse. Your journey on the Trail ends here.

THE END

It's a very hard decision, but you can't give up any more of your water rations to oxen, not while you're lost in the desert. You'll be two oxen down, but four oxen will still be able to pull your wagon.

"Eh, excuse me." Fergus leans against the side of your wagon. "But I think there's somethin' ye need t' know. I saw someone stealin' yer water the other night, when ye were all sleepin'."

"It would make sense." Mama looks to Papa, worried. "We've been so careful about measuring out our rations. It was either a leak, or . . ."

Papa stands up. "Did you see who it was?"

Fergus points to the Beauregard wagon. "It was the Cap'n's son. George. Saw him carryin' it in buckets."

Your eyes widen.

"What should we do?" Mama puts her hand on

your shoulder. "If his parents don't know about it, then we can't really say much. He's just a child. If they're lacking water—"

"And if they do know about it?" Papa's brow furrows. "Either way, we're all down on our water rations. He's old enough to know that he's stealing—and stealing something that could mean the difference between life and death."

Mama shakes her head. "So what should we do?"

Should you confront the Beauregards about their son stealing water, or say nothing?

To confront the Beauregards, turn to page **83**

To say nothing, turn to page **56**

Papa is far away from you, but you still think it's a better idea to call him back for help.

"Papa! Papa, help! Snake!"

"Hang on!" Papa hurries back. "Don't move!"

 Tippet barks wildly. The snake briefly turns its attention to your foxhound, lashing out at Tippet's nose. Tippet snaps back at the snake and tries to bat at it with a paw.

You dash away and into Papa's arms. The snake nearly gets Tippet's paw, but the dog's sharp teeth make the snake recede into the grass.

"Tippet, c'mere!" You pat your leg. Tippet ignores you for a minute, but finally trots away from the snake and stares up at you dolefully.

Papa catches the snake. "It's not much, but it's something."

It's not quite the meal you were hoping for, but it's a bit of protein.

You're so hungry sitting by the campfire that you can hardly wait for the snake meat to finish cooking.

You dig into your slim piece of snake before the others. Mama warns you that the meat might not be fully cooked. In the back of your mind, you know that eating undercooked food might make you sick, but you're too hungry to care.

That night, you wake up to stomach cramps and severe nausea. You die of food poisoning within the next day.

 **THE END**

Spot will throw you as soon as you try to mount him. It's not a good idea to ride him right now. You'll have to round up the livestock on foot.

You made the right call. Spot kicks out at anything that gets near him for the rest of the day. Finally, you stop for supper. You're so tired, you can't even think about eating, but when you smell smoked meat, you force yourself to stay awake. You help Mama make cornbread.

Mr. Southworth walks over with his fiddle case and a bag of coffee to join your family for supper again. He wears suspenders and a bright blue shirt, and he's whistling a joyful tune. The McAllisters also bring food, and three children. Fiona and Harry are twelve and ten—around your age—and have bright red hair with faces covered in freckles—just like their father. The third child is a tiny babe with red curls sprouting from her little head. Despite everyone's exhaustion, laughter rings out through your campsite.

"Here." Mr. Southworth hands you a steaming tin cup of coffee. "Think you could use this."

"Thanks." The bitter coffee burns your throat, but you like the chicory taste. You see Harry trying a sip across the fire. He makes a face, and you share grins.

"I don't think I ever asked—what made you folks decide to come out West?" Mr. Southworth sips his coffee. "Has the gold fever struck you, too?"

There's a distance in your mother's expression. "In a way. It's time for a fresh start. Connecticut has been growing more crowded by the day. The land has been taken away from us bit by bit, tree by tree. My people, the Mashantucket Pequots, were either sold off as slaves or forced to barter over the tiniest bit of reservation. Many of my family have left the reservation to find work. My brother and his wife moved out to California several years ago, and we're considering joining them in Sacramento—or going to Oregon City. We haven't decided yet."

"I've got hope for the future." Mr. Southworth checks his pocket watch and snaps it shut. "It's been hard, I'm not going to lie. But I plan on buying freedom for myself and my mother once I reach her in Oregon. I've dreamt about it my whole life, and it's so close now I can just taste it." He scratches his thick beard, his eyes growing wistful. "With a little blacksmithing here, some gold mining there. I plan on farming, too. And maybe with a bit of this gold nugget right here." He pulls out his fiddle case. "Anything to give my mother and I the freedom we deserve."

Your eyes widen. "You're going to play the fiddle?"

He laughs. "That's right. Folk of all kinds pay to hear good music. And that's what I play: good music." He plucks at the strings before picking up his bow.

He starts to play, and a sweet sound emerges from the fiddle. His fingers dance over the strings as he swipes the bow back and forth. You recognize the tune as "Turkey in the Straw."

"It's magical!" Fiona tosses a coin into the fiddle case and gets up to dance. Eventually she drags you, Benji, and a reluctant Harry along, and soon enough everyone is clapping to Mr. Southworth's lively music. It's a joyful finish to a difficult couple of days.

In the morning, you set off for Red Vermillion Crossing. You roll through flat plains and gentle hills. It takes two and a half days.

"Another river crossing?" You ride Spot alongside the wagon. "Didn't we just ford a river?"

Papa nods. "We'll have to cross a lot of rivers to get where we're going. But believe me—if we end up going on the California Trail, we'll be wishing we were crossing rivers every week. We'll be in the worst stretch of desert you can imagine."

Your mouth already feels dry. "Maybe we should go to Oregon City instead."

"Maybe so." Papa wipes his brow.

When you come to the toll bridge operator, you find that it costs one dollar per wagon to cross. Your wagon train halts, arguing over options.

"It's a fortune." Papa puts his hands on his hips. "But to ford the river might cost us even more in the end."

"There may be another way." Mama looks closely at the map.

"We could follow the Vermillion River north until it narrows into a creek and cross there. It'll add several days to our journey. Keep in mind: More time means we need more food to eat."

It's a tough decision. Should you pay the toll and risk not having enough money for the rest of the trip? Or go around the toll and add time onto your trip? What should you do?

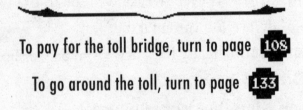

To pay for the toll bridge, turn to page **108**

To go around the toll, turn to page **133**

The wagons are heavily damaged and will take too long to repair, even with Mr. Southworth and Papa working together to fix them. The bandits might come back or the weather could get worse and flood the chasm. You need to help everyone walk back toward Fort Hall to get them out of danger.

You help a wounded person walk as Papa puts two small children on Spot. Mr. Southworth's horse carries three other children. It's a long, slow slog back to your camp at American Falls with frequent rest stops.

Everyone is tired, hungry, and irritable. You don't have a doctor in your wagon train, but Mama steps in to help with her knowledge of splinting broken bones.

The stranded pioneers lost most of their food

supply to the bandits, and they're far too tired to go hunting for food themselves. You and Mr. Southworth share what you can spare, but it's hardly enough, and you have to think about your own families for the coming difficult months ahead on the Trail. What's more, some people in your wagon train don't want the extra burden of these new pioneers.

You're faced with a new dilemma: Should you bring the stranded pioneers all the way back to Fort Hall, or take them with you?

To bring them back to Fort Hall, turn to page **31**

To take them with you, turn to page **79**

It's not a good idea." You get closer to Papa. "Why would they share their 'secret' gold stash? It doesn't make sense, does it?"

Papa slowly shakes his head. "No, it doesn't." He draws the other members of your wagon train aside. While John seems intent on wanting to believe them, you see doubt creep into the others' eyes. Finally, John relents and agrees with you and Papa.

As you leave the fur trappers behind, you see their angry, resentful glares. You made the right call.

The next day, your wagon train moves on from Fort Laramie. You travel through the heart of the Great Plains. Just when you think you'll never see another hill again, you find yourselves passing small but steadily increasing slopes. You're nearing the mountains—and South Pass.

You make it to Independence Rock on July tenth, only several days after Independence Day. Your wagon train stops to have a little celebration. Even though you stocked up on flour, beans, and bacon back at Fort Laramie, you still have trouble finding buffalo herds. You use every buffalo chip sparingly and make it last as long as possible.

Your wagon train comes to an infamous rocky gorge called Devil's Gate, a gorge too narrow to fit a single wagon through.

Harry puts his hand to your ear. "I heard that there was a murder here. That's why people call this place Devil's Gate—they think it's haunted."

You smack your lips. "Just a tall tale."

Harry shrugs. "I read it in a pamphlet somewhere."

Even Fiona looks uneasy as you stop to rest near

a trading post at Devil's Gate. You still carve your names into the rock and make note of the bighorn sheep climbing atop the crags. You try not to be too concerned about how low the Sweetwater River has become. You're in a drought, and it's a not a good sign for your time ahead in the desert.

A day after leaving Devil's Gate, Mr. Southworth and Papa spot another buffalo herd nearby and go off to hunt. You stick around to help prepare the camp for the night. That night, a hearty celebration takes place when Mr. Southworth and Papa come back with a buffalo. You eat your fill of the meat.

The next day, you sneak another piece of buffalo

meat from the night before onto the skillet. Mama's always told you it's bad to eat meat that's been sitting—even if you cook it. But you know that johnnycakes and bacon won't fill you up.

After you eat the buffalo, you don't feel well. You sneak back to your wagon and take a sip of some medicine Mama brought. You feel better almost right away, but not entirely. You want to drink more, but Mama warned against taking too much. But maybe a little more couldn't hurt? Should you take more, or be patient and wait for it to work?

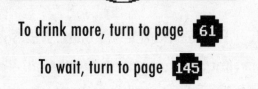

To drink more, turn to page **61**

To wait, turn to page **145**

You let the stranded pioneers join your wagon train. The additional folks diminish your supplies more quickly, but you have to help them get to Oregon City. The rest of your wagon train isn't happy with the decision.

As you start off, your pace is much slower than you'd anticipated. With the wounded and children adding weight to the wagons, you and Mr. Southworth lag behind the rest of your wagon train. It's like you're moving through quicksand.

Everyone else becomes impatient and picks up their pace. You can't keep up. When you finally reach Three Island Crossing, exhausted and out of

supplies, your family decides to stop your journey here. You set up a way station for fellow pioneers and live off of trading. It's not Oregon City, but you and your family have a decent life here.

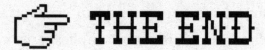 **THE END**

You hold off on eating and drinking. You take one sip of water that's been boiled. Instead of joining your family for supper, you crawl into the tent you share with Benji and try to rest.

"What's the matter?" Mama pokes her head into the tent and presses her hand on your forehead. "You're burning up and your skin is clammy. What did you eat today? Were you bitten by something?" She hurries to check the back of your neck and the rest of your body for bites.

"No, I . . . I think it was the . . . water." The inside of the tent spins around you.

"Let us hope you don't have dysentery." Mama rubs your back and rushes to get you a tin cup of boiled water. "Here. Sip slowly. You can't become dehydrated."

Over the next couple of days, several other members of the wagon train become sick as well, including Papa.

"The water could be brackish or alkaline." Mama

helps Papa climb into the wagon to rest. "We need to make sure all water is boiled before drinking."

Your wagon train crawls into Alcove Spring at a snail's pace. Papa lies in the back of the wagon, pale and sweaty. You ride on Spot, hunched over in pain and weak. You can't herd the livestock feeling this sick.

You rest in Alcove Spring for several days. The rest of the wagon train is too far ahead to help. Soon enough, all of you are too weak to continue on the Trail.

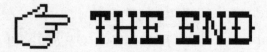 **THE END**

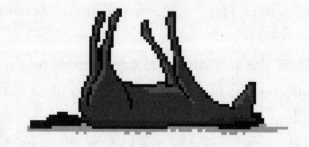

You confront the Beauregards. John and Stella are horrified at the news.

"We had no idea." Dark bags hang under John's eyes. "He will apologize."

Papa straightens his hat. "We're *all* suffering out here, John."

"I know." John sighs heavily. "I'm beginning to think we shouldn't have taken this *cutoff.*"

"We could always try to go back." Mama wipes her face on her dress. "Salt Lake City isn't that far from here. If we cut down our rations even more, we can make our way back up to Fort Hall and possibly start again on the California Trail from there. We'll have the Humboldt River most of the way across the desert that way. Or we go northwest to Oregon City."

You have no other choice. You'll backtrack toward

Salt Lake City and up to Fort Hall. Maybe you'll run into Mr. Southworth? Maybe you'll end up going to Oregon City instead of California, after all.

Turn back to page **32**

You go back and ford the river. The water is higher by this point, but you'd rather risk the river crossing than keep going without any water supply. Your animals won't make it without more water—neither will you. At your current pace, you'll be lucky to make it five miles in one day in these sluggish muddy hills.

When you finally return to Carlin Canyon, the river is even higher than you'd anticipated.

Slowly your wagon train attempts to ford the river. But when Beauregard's wagon hits a slippery rock and sinks down into a strong current, the rest of you are quick to follow in the chaos. Everyone is swept away in the gushing river.

☞ THE END

You stay at Rancho Johnson to search for more gold. Fiona and Harry argue over whether you should keep the nugget a secret from the owners of the ranch. Harry says that you should keep it. Fiona says that it's not your land and the nugget doesn't belong to you.

In the end, you keep the nugget for yourself.

That evening you show Mama and Papa your incredible discovery. They're both astounded and suspicious at once.

"Where did you find that?" Mama's brow furrows. "If you found that on this land, you need to return it—now."

"Your mother's right." Papa puts his hand on your shoulder. "First thing in the morning. It's the right thing to do."

Benji tries to grab the nugget; you pocket it quickly.

Your parents are right.

In the morning you return the nugget, much to

the astonishment and happiness of the owners. So thankful that you're honest, they offer to let your parents stay and open a trading post on an enormous plot of land nearby to aid passing pioneers and gold-seekers. Your parents aren't sure at first, but the offer seems too good to pass up.

Your mother's brother and his family live close by in Sacramento, so you'll be able to visit them often. You may have not reached your original final destination of Sacramento, but it's close enough. You'll do just fine here.

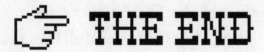 **THE END**

Even with his carpentry skills, Papa can't fix the wagon on his own.

You pull Papa aside. "We should take Mr. Southworth up on his offer and have him stay. We can't get stuck out here alone."

Papa rubs his temples. "Are you sure you don't mind, Mr. Southworth?"

Mr. Southworth smiles. "I'm happy to stay. Strength in numbers, right? Plus, you'd all miss the sound of my fiddle too much." He winks at you.

You grin. "You know it!"

Mr. Southworth easily replaces the axle and helps Papa fit a new wheel into place with spare parts you've brought along. It's perfectly round and shiny, glossy with grease on its iron rim. The wagon rolls so much more smoothly now.

That night, you camp in the rolling slopes near

 South Pass, trying to forget that you're a mere two-wagon train corralled out here in the vast wilderness. As you help Mama prepare dinner, you hear coyotes in the distance. A shiver runs up your spine. Tippet lets out a bark in return.

"We'll have to take turns being on guard duty tonight, Mr. Southworth." Papa warms his hands by the campfire. "Without the others to help, we're on our own for tonight. I'm worried about the livestock."

Mr. Southworth takes a seat on a rock by the fire. "We can rotate in four-hour periods."

"Will the wolves get us?" Benji holds on to Mama.

Mr. Southworth exchanges smiles with Mama and pulls out his fiddle. "C'mon now, little man. This sweet melody will protect us." He plays a warm, soft tune that calms Benji.

"I can help go on guard duty." You hand Papa dirty dishes to clean after supper.

Papa hesitates. "Not tonight, I'm afraid. I'll need your help to herd the livestock tomorrow. Riding Spot takes all the energy you've got."

He's right. But as you try to drift off to sleep to the sound of Mr. Southworth's fiddle, you still hear coyotes shriek. And they sound like they're coming closer. You don't get much sleep that night.

South Pass is such a gentle area of terrain that you hardly realize you're in mountain country. In the distance you see the hint of blue-capped peaks rising into the horizon, but you soon pass into sandier, flatter terrain. Finally, you spot a number of wagons in the distance. Relief overwhelms you: it's your wagon train! You haven't fallen that far behind. You're so glad to join up with Fiona and Harry again.

The Parting of Ways." Mama reads from her map. "Some people go to California this way, past Salt Lake City. I've heard the salt flats around there are really something."

"The first emigrants to come this way were the Bidwell-Bartleson party." Harry peers over another anatomy book to join the conversation. "They split off at Soda Springs to California on the Bidwell-Bartleson Route."

"That's right." Mama folds up her map and sticks it in her apron pocket. "And John Bidwell's the one that led them."

Your reunion with the wagon train doesn't last long. Some people, including John Beauregard, have been reading the guidebook of Lansford Hastings, an explorer and guide who created the Hastings Cutoff to California through the Salt Lake Desert. Beauregard and several other wagons want to try that route instead staying on this route toward Fort Hall.

You're not sure what to do. You've heard the name Hastings before, but not in a good way. The Hastings Cutoff might shave time off your journey. What do you decide?

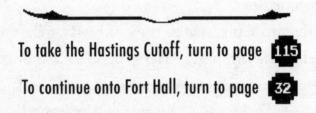

To take the Hastings Cutoff, turn to page **115**

To continue onto Fort Hall, turn to page **32**

You keep going. You've already started on the Greenhorn Cutoff, and with all the rain that's accumulated, you know that the river will be far too high to cross. After all, it's only about five miles until you reach the cutoff that joins back up with the California Trail and the Humboldt River. You think you can make it a day without a water supply.

But without the sight of the river and with the trail ahead destroyed by the monsoon, the road ahead becomes murky. John Beauregard tries to find the cutoff trail, but by the end of the day, there is no river in sight. You should have reached the river junction several miles ago. You're wandering around in the desert hills, lost and without water. You won't make it out of the desert.

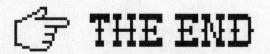 **THE END**

You split up and plan to rejoin the rest of the wagon train at the end of the cutoff. Your family isn't happy with the idea, but you also don't want any other wagons to get stuck in the mud. You watch them struggle over the next muddy hill and disappear. Rain beats down on you, soaking your clothes.

You and Mama help Papa steady the wagon enough so he can replace the broken wheel. It's a long, arduous process that takes every bit of strength you have. As the day wears on, you discover that the wheels are only sinking *deeper* into the mud. One of your goats sinks halfway into a mud pit—quicksand!

Now your whole wagon sinks deeper. Neither your family nor your oxen are strong enough to tow it out. You're stuck here in the desert hills—forever.

☞ **THE END**

You go on with Mr. Southworth to Oregon City in a ten-wagon train. You can't risk traveling through the desert with this current drought. You can always move down to California later—there's plenty of gold mining in Oregon City.

You wave goodbye to John Beauregard and the other wagons and start off for the next landmark on the Oregon Trail: American Falls, on the Snake River. Near the rushing waterfall is a narrow passage through the rocks called the Gate of Death.

When you were at Fort Hall, traders told you the River Rush Gang lurks all along this part of the Trail. Mr. Southworth decides to scout the route ahead. Papa offers to let him use Spot to make the journey quicker.

"He can be stubborn at first, but don't worry."

You pat Spot. "He'll ease up once you ride together for a little."

Much to your surprise, Spot doesn't give Mr. Southworth any trouble.

"Maybe he just likes my fiddle playing." Mr. Southworth laughs. He tips his hat and rides off ahead, disappearing into the horizon.

Several hours later, Mr. Southworth enters the wagon corral at a gallop. "There's a wagon train stranded at the Gate of Death. They're in a bad way. We should go help them out before bandits get to them."

Some people in your wagon train don't want to help the stranded people. The odds of running into the River Rush Gang would be much greater.

"I'll go with you." Papa pulls on his boots. "It's not a one-man job, that's for certain."

"This is not a good idea." Fergus McAllister recedes back to his wagon.

Although Papa wants to help, the threat of the River Rush Gang ambushing this vulnerable wagon train is very real. Should you help the pioneers in need, or steer clear?

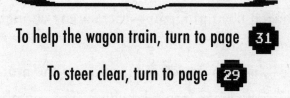

To help the wagon train, turn to page **31**

To steer clear, turn to page **29**

You try to repair the wagons. It'll take too much time and effort to wrangle everyone, especially with so many wounded people who can't walk.

Papa and Mr. Southworth replace the wheels and axles. Soon, they discover that most of the wagons are damaged beyond repair—there aren't enough replacement parts.

"We'll have to decide what to do in the morning." Papa blows his nose into a kerchief. "For tonight, we'll have to stick it out here."

That night, you camp in the open air and sleep uneasily near the steep rock chasm. You jolt awake. The ground moves underneath you. A roaring sound rushes through your ears.

"Flood!" Mr. Southworth starts to run to higher ground. "Get to higher ground!"

But it's too late. Water and rocks rush through the chasm and carry everyone away.

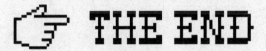 **THE END**

You don't shoot the gun. If the gun scares the buffalo, you risk a stampede—which won't end well. You are confident that you'll find other game to hunt on your journey.

"C'mon, Benji." You grab his hand. "Let's find Papa."

When you reunite with Papa and Mr. Southworth, you tell them about the buffalo. Papa agrees you made the right call.

"That would've been a foolhardy move, trying to shoot with that small pistol. We'll go back and tell the others about the herd." Papa puts his hands in his pockets, turning on his heel.

After hours of patient hunting, Mr. Southworth and Papa work together to take down a buffalo. You all share a very hearty supper, thankful for the buffalo, and you've got enough food now to last for at least another week. Mama saves its shaggy hide to sew into a coat later. She drops a dried dung patty into the fire pit and ignites the campfire.

"Buffalo chips burn well." She throws a log onto the roaring fire. "We need to find as many of these as we can. Kindling is a precious commodity on the Trail."

Fiona McAllister skips over to your campfire, dragging her reluctant brother Harry in tow. You've befriended both of them, despite how different they are. Fiona is a daredevil and likes to ride her family's mustang. Harry prefers reading to anything else. He's already talking about going to medical school. The three of you play games along the way and set up camp with their family and Mr. Southworth at night.

You take a seat by the fire between Harry and Fiona. "So why's your family going out West?"

"Our da's not going for the Gold Rush, like so many others." Harry throws a twig into the fire. "He's going because he doesn't like the cold."

Your stare at him. "But . . . surely you don't have to go thousands of miles to get somewhere warm."

Harry shrugs and looks at Fiona.

Fiona rolls her eyes. "Don't listen to Harry. We're

going out West because Da wants his own farm. Land wasn't really available back East, y'know?"

You nod.

You don't remember being this excited in your life. Fort Kearney, which you stopped at many miles ago, even before passing Courthouse and Jailhouse Rock, feels like forever ago. Fort Laramie is a bustling den of soldiers, fur trappers, Native Nations, and plenty of pioneers.

Mr. Southworth immediately finds a ready audience for his expert fiddle-playing. Entertaining hopeful gold-seekers on their way to California and Oregon, he plays all day, and in the end, coins in his fiddle case almost spill over.

"Maybe I don't even need to pan for gold at all. Maybe this is all the gold I really need." He holds up his fiddle proudly.

As you wander around the bustling fort, you come across John, Fergus, Papa, and a few other members of your wagon train talking to a few men.

Papa gets closer to you and pulls his kerchief over his mouth. "They're fur trappers who claim to have found a secret gold stash nearby. John and Fergus want to check it out. What do you think?"

You're thrilled that Papa is asking for your advice—and you don't want to steer him wrong.

One of the fur trappers steps into your space. "All we need are a few good men to come help us mine it."

There's something off about these guys. Why would they want to share a secret stash of gold with you and your wagon train? But what if there's a fortune that'll make you all rich?

Should you tell Papa to go with the fur trappers, or convince him otherwise?

To convince him not to go, turn to page **75**

To check out the gold stash, turn to page **19**

You turn back and go home. It's already dangerous enough to travel across the Oregon–California Trail with a wagon train; without one, it's asking for trouble. Lone wagons rarely make it.

You try to regain your sense of direction and turn back toward Independence. Clouds hang low in the sky, and a cool, dry wind sweeps across the plains. Lightning strikes and a heavy rain pours down, bouncing off your wagon's oiled canvas cover. Even the hat you've been wearing doesn't help keep the rain away.

But then something hits you on the back of the neck.

"Ow!" Did Benji throw a rock at you?

"Hail!" Papa dives into the wagon. "C'mon! Get under cover, quick!"

Chunks of hail plummet from the sky. Soon the canvas can't take it, and hailstones rip through your wagon top, destroying everything. You won't be going any farther on the Trail now.

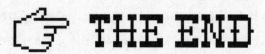 **THE END**

You've come this far and you're confident that you'll find your way out of these prairielands and get back on the Trail.

But there's another problem. During the dust storm, your livestock has run off, leaving you without goat's milk and emergency food. You have some bacon and flour left, but you were counting on getting to Fort Laramie with your wagon train to restock.

As you try to continue on through the dust-covered landscape, clouds cover the sky. Thunder rumbles across the plains. The storm will pass, you hope, but instead it continues for days. You're really lost.

You wander around the prairielands for weeks. Papa and Tippet hunt for smaller game like prairie dogs and jackrabbits, but it's just not enough. You run out of food. Your trek on the Trail ends here.

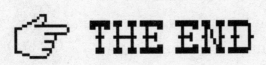 THE END

You're already going slow due to the large number of wagons in your train. You're barely covering fifteen miles a day. To go miles around the toll bridge will cost you more time than it's worth.

You tug on Papa's shirt. "We should pay the toll. After all, we'll be hunting for food along the way, and with your carpentry and Mr. Southworth's blacksmith skills, we save money on wagon repair fees."

Papa nods. "True enough." He glances at Mama. "What do you think?"

"Bridge, bridge." Benji jumps on the wagon seat beside Mama.

"You and Mukki are right." Mama smiles. "Let's cross the bridge."

After some debate among the families, all forty wagons agree to pay the toll and cross the Vermillion River. As you continue on into the prairielands, you have a lot of great conversations with Mr. Southworth and get to know him better.

You run into a few other wagon

trains and camps along the way, all headed to California or Oregon for the Gold Rush. Mr. Southworth plays his fiddle for them and returns later at night, just before the guards go on duty, his pockets and fiddle case full of money.

You love Mr. Southworth's music lulling you to sleep. It even helps soothe Benji into slumber, and that's a hard thing to do.

The next morning, a new concern arises among the members of the wagon train: lack of game. Rabbits and prairie dogs can be caught every now and then, but the major source of food along the Trail, buffalo, have been scarce.

You go out one afternoon with Papa, Mr. Southworth, and Benji to scout for buffalo ahead of the wagon train. You are sure to put a small pistol in your holster in case you see some game. As you scan the horizon, you're jarred by the quiet. Then it hits you: You haven't heard your brother's voice for some time.

"Wait." You tense up. "Where's Benji?"

You all look around. He was right behind you just a second ago.

"He can't have gone far." Papa is frantically scanning the landscape. "Everyone spread out. Take Tippet with you."

You rush off across the plains, searching. Tippet bounds at your heels. You clamber up a hill, then halt, fear gripping your heart.

A short distance away, you see a group of men on horses. As you approach, one of the men motions to the others, and the circle of horses parts to reveal a dirt-covered Benji.

"Benji!" You rush into the circle and hug him. "You can't wander off like that!"

"He would have gotten lost on these plains." The man sits on a spotted horse and points to the hills. "We surrounded him to protect him."

"Thank you." You give Benji's hand a squeeze. Benji looks up. "You look like Mama."

Your cheeks grow hot. "They're not Pequot, Mukki."

"We are Neshnabé. Or Pottawatomi, to the white people. I am Nikan." He nods to you.

"We're Pequot, from back East. Thank you again." A sudden thought strikes you. "Uh, excuse me. Why haven't we seen any buffalo around these parts?"

"Buffalo have been scarce." Nikan frowns. "It has rained very little this season. When you find a herd, do not hunt greedily."

They wish you luck and ride off into the distance. You and Benji hurry back to find Papa and Mr. Southworth. But instead, you find yourselves staring at a small herd of buffalo grazing on the prairie. You've got the pistol on your hip. Should you try to kill a buffalo now, or wait for Papa and Mr.

Southworth? The buffalo might stampede. But what if the buffalo wander off and you can't find them again? What do you decide?

To get Papa first, turn to page **100**

To shoot the buffalo now, turn to page **21**

You ask the rest of the wagon train to stay with you and help Papa fix the broken wheel. The last thing you want is to be left behind in the middle of the desert during a monsoon. They agree to stay, but the situation only gets worse. Several of the other wagons have to be towed out of the mud. In the chaos, supplies are lost and damaged, including your water. Everyone is irritable and soaking wet.

Finally, they manage to pull your wagon and a few of your animals out of the mud. You lose one goat. Papa and the others fix the wheel, but you've lost days of travel time. Your food and water supplies are dangerously low. The McAllisters spare some water for your family, but it's not much.

The rain finally stops two days later. The muddy earth begins to dry. You've still got about five miles to go until you reach the river junction. Should you turn around and try to ford Carlin Canyon or keep pressing on?

To go back, turn to page **85**

To keep going, turn to page **93**

You move toward the Hastings Cutoff past Salt Lake City on the California Trail. After all, it's quicker according to the map in the guidebook. Instead of staying northwest on the Oregon Trail, the Hastings Cutoff starts down past Fort Bridger and runs right through Salt Lake City. You'll shave some time off your trip by going through the Salt Lake Desert.

Some members in the wagon train don't want to take the cutoff. Mr. Southworth will head toward Oregon City. After a tearful farewell with Mr. Southworth, you leave with half of your wagon train for Fort Bridger.

You save money for supplies until you reach Salt Lake City, where your wagon train rests and stocks up. Two days later, you roll off west across a sandbar that abuts a body of water that looks like a mirror: the Great Salt Lake. In the distance, majestic mountains rise in jagged peaks on the horizon.

It's so breathtaking a sight that you almost want

to go back to Salt Lake City and live there, just to be near the lake. But you continue on and find yourselves across the flat white stretch of sand and salt.

"The salt flats." Papa points to the ground. "Nothing quite like it."

You couldn't agree more. Your eyes are nearly blinded by the reflection of the sun on the pristine white ground.

When you stop for nooning, you see Benji reach down and bury his wet finger in the sand. You reach

out to try to stop Benji from licking his salty finger. "Uh . . . don't—"

Benji giggles. "Yummy!"

As the days pass in the endless desert, the mountains always seem just out of reach.

"We're going in circles." Mama smacks the sides of her hips.

Papa shakes his head. "That's not our only problem. Two of our oxen aren't looking good. We've been driving them too hard. We'll need to give them some more of our water rations or . . ."

It clicks. He means to put down the oxen to save water.

You want to keep the oxen alive and well, but you also want to keep your family alive. You're torn. What do you decide?

To give the oxen more water, turn to page **131**

To put the oxen down to save your water, turn to page **63**

You've just met Jim Beckwourth, but you have a good feeling about him and his alternate route. Your mother does too, and you trust her judgment. Plus, you've heard that the Carson Route will take you through challenging mountain terrain.

You look at your parents. "We should go with him."

Benji stuffs half a piece of bacon into his mouth. Tippet snatches the rest of it out of his hand and licks his fingers.

"I agree with you and your mother." Papa's skin has been sunburnt for days now because of the hot sun. He wipes his dusty brow. "Anything that will make our trip easier is fine with me."

You say goodbye to the Beauregards, who have ultimately turned out to be good wagon train captains. They separate with over half of the wagon train to continue on the Carson Route, leaving you with a ten-wagon train. You're happy the McAllisters are still traveling with you.

Jim Beckwourth leads the way on his horse. *He's a great storyteller,* you think, as he recounts his life experiences. Born a slave to his African American mother and her white master, he was first trained as a blacksmith, gained his freedom and eventually made his way west, working as a wrangler, a fur trapper, and a soldier. "I'm a mountain man, through and through." He weaves tales of adventures of living with a village in the Crow Nation. "They captured me and thought that I was the lost son of their chief. I became a war chief and married the old chief's daughter. Matter of fact, most folks think I'm Crow."

"Do you consider yourself more Crow, then, Mr. Beckwourth?" Mama's eyebrow angles.

"I wouldn't say that necessarily, although the Crow have taken me in."

As you make your way northwest, you come to the Truckee River and stop to replenish your water supplies. From there, you divert onto the Beckwourth Trail, a smooth path for your wagon wheels. As you continue northwest, the desert-scape begins to return to greener sagebrush; sandy ground to harder dirt and scrub grass; and even scraggly pine trees appear on the horizon.

You stop at a place called Peavine Springs to stock up on water. As you pass by, you see an odd white lake in the distance.

"White Lake." Mr. Beckwourth points. "It's a dry lake, so don't get your hopes up."

You continue through gentle hills of sagebrush into the Sierra Valley. You've entered California, Mr. Beckwourth tells you. Going deeper into the valley, you come across the Feather River, where your wagon train corrals for the night. Mama is especially excited to fish and catches several fat trout and a catfish. You roast the fish over the fire for dinner.

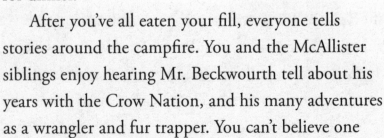

After you've all eaten your fill, everyone tells stories around the campfire. You and the McAllister siblings enjoy hearing Mr. Beckwourth tell about his years with the Crow Nation, and his many adventures as a wrangler and fur trapper. You can't believe one man has experienced so much in one lifetime, and it makes you want to do the same. You've missed sweet fiddle tunes lulling you to slumber each night, but going to bed full of fish and stories helps you sleep a bit better.

The next morning, you wind your way north into the wooded territory of Grizzly Creek. It's so wonderful to finally be under shaded trees again—it reminds you of the oaks back home in Connecticut. In the lush meadows of Grizzly Valley, you enjoy fishing, hunting, and the cool, crisp waters of the nearby creek.

Grizzly Ridge is the only particularly steep terrain of the journey thus far, and takes careful maneuvering to traverse. As Papa walks alongside the oxen, you lead Spot and the livestock. Going down the ridge is another matter: it's far too steep to simply lead the wagons down. Mr. Beckwourth helps your wagon train cut down giant logs. You rope them to the back of the wagons to slow their descent.

In the valley, you spot a lot of gold mining

camps. You weave through more wooded summits and valleys as you descend into Marysville, a tiny town consisting of ranchers and miners. A post office has just been established, and the town just elected a mayor. You rest in Marysville for a couple days. Two of the wagons stay there to mine gold.

You part ways with Mr. Beckwourth and thank him profusely. He promises to stop by to visit your family in Sacramento soon. You're going to miss traveling with him.

On your way down to Sacramento, you stop to rest briefly at an adobe house called Rancho Johnson. While your parents are talking to the owners, you and the McAllister siblings wander off to explore nearby.

As you climb on some boulders, you see a flash of gold hidden in a crevice. Reaching down, you pull out a glittering golden rock.

"A gold nugget!" Harry's eyes widen behind his glasses. "Quick, hide it in your pocket."

"What if there's more?" Fiona digs around near where you found the nugget.

You've struck gold here near Rancho Johnson, but does that mean you should give up your goal of reaching Sacramento to mine for gold here? What should you do?

To stay near Rancho Johnson, turn to page **86**

To go to Sacramento, turn to page **150**

You stay at Lone Elm Campground despite
Fergus's warnings. Your parents don't want to drive
the animals any further. Too much, and they'll be
exhausted. To lose your team of oxen at the start
of the Trail would be devastating. The wagon train
captain, John Beauregard, is also cautious to risk such
a venture on hearsay.

"One night can't hurt us." John blots his face
with a kerchief. "If we do run into bandits later, we'll
be able to fight them off fully energized and alert.
I don't see how they'd come after us here, not with
all of these other wagons corralled nearby. It'd be a
foolhardy attempt—just like it would be foolhardy
for us to try to round everyone up right now."

"We also have night guards on watch." Papa wipes
the dark circles under his eyes.

You're worried about the River Rush Gang, but
you reluctantly agree. Fergus McAllister, on the other
hand, refuses to accept John Beauregard's decision.

"Ye cannot be serious. Yer puttin' all of us a' risk,
Beauregard!" Fergus storms off into the night. Soon

after, you see his wagon rolling off into the dark. You're sad—you know he has children your age. You hope you'll run into them later along the Trail and be friends.

You and your parents go back to your camp, confident. But then you feel a lump in your throat— the uneasiness makes it hard to fall asleep.

You're jolted by the frightening sounds of gunshots, shouting, and your foxhound, Tippet, barking. You scramble out of your tent and tell Benji to stay inside. Your camp is filled with bandits! They round up everyone in the wagon corral and steal everyone's money. Now you have nothing left for your trip out West. You have to turn around to Independence and find work there—if you can make it back.

 **THE END**

It's better to be safe than sorry. You need to convince the others to leave now before the bandits arrive.

You step forward. "But what about the bandits, Mr. Beauregard? Shouldn't we try to keep everyone safe?"

Everyone turns to look at you.

John Beauregard runs a hand over his thick mustache. "Yes. It could just be rumors, kid."

"Or maybe not." Mr. Southworth steps out of the crowd. "Back in Independence, I overheard that the local sheriff had a warrant out for the notorious River Rush Gang who was out robbing pioneers all along the Trail. We shouldn't take chances."

John scratches his chin.

"Mr. Southworth's right, Mr. Beauregard." Everyone's eyes are on you again. "We should leave now before they catch up with us."

Finally, John nods and rises to his feet. "All right. Can't risk bandits on my first night out as wagon train captain. Fergus, you sound the bugle. Let's round everyone up and get moving."

As you roll out, you see George Beauregard grumbling about not getting to finish supper. You hear the bugle and see the families pause from their supper, startled by the alarm.

"Everyone, listen up!" John stands on the driver's seat of his wagon. "I need everyone to pack up and get ready to move—now!"

A wave of murmurs trills through the wagon train.

"I know everyone's settled down." John puts his hands to his mouth. "But we've heard talk of bandits nearby. Unless you want to risk getting robbed blind, I suggest you do as I say."

You and Papa hurry back to your wagon and help Mama and Benji pack and round up your livestock. Within the hour, your wagon train drags off to a slow crawl. Only the stars guide you in the dark.

It'll be about sixty miles to your next major

crossing: Pappan's Ferry at the Kansas River. It'll be a long and slow trek. At your current pace, you're barely going fifteen miles a day. It doesn't help that no one's had a full night's rest—not even your animals. You walk all night and finally stop to rest briefly for breakfast, then again for the midday "nooning" bugle. Your eyelids droop as the warm afternoon sun bears down on your face. You shake yourself awake several times. Your feet drag.

It takes over four days to get to Pappan's Ferry. The ferry is too expensive, so you choose to ford the Kansas River. One by one your wagons make it through the rushing river. Several wagons are damaged in the crossing, but Mr. Southworth helps to fix them, being an experienced blacksmith.

The next morning, you wake to the sound of your horse, Spot, pawing at the ground. The wind picks up and blows storm clouds across the sky.

"The animals are restless." Mama covers the back of the wagon. "A storm's coming in. It's good we crossed the river earlier. You'll need to keep a close eye on the herd."

You pull your boots on. "I can ride Spot, Mama. It'll help herd the animals more easily."

"Your father barely got him on the ferry, and the storm won't help his foul temperament. We should walk him a little further, I think."

"I'll be careful."

As you approach, Spot rears up and tosses his head. His ears flick back against his head, a sure sign that he won't like it if you try to get near him, much less ride him.

"C'mon, Spotty." Spot snaps at your outstretched hand.

You step back. Your feet are blistered and sore beyond belief. The thought of having to herd the

animals on foot is pure misery. But trying to ride
Spot right now might not be the best idea either.
What should you do?

To try to ride Spot, turn to page **24**

To keep going on foot, turn to page **67**

You give the two oxen some of your water rations to save them. You'll find more water sources in the mountains—if you can escape these salt flats.

The oxen slurp up the water quickly in the extreme heat. You feel the sun radiating off the white salt flat sands. Your mouth is so dry. You go to drink the rest of the water in your canteen. It's empty.

You don't have enough for Spot. He's struggled to carry you and Papa through the desert, his tongue hanging out and hooves dragging through the sand.

The next morning, Spot is lying on his back, unmoving. Your beloved stubborn horse is the first casualty on the California Trail. Tears and sand stick to your face—Benji's, too. Not long after, you lose a goat and your only sheep. You have a feeling you're next.

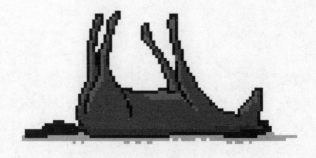

Your six oxen need too much water to survive, and now your family doesn't have enough. No one else in the wagon train can spare any, and by the time you reach the mountains, it'll be too late. Your journey on the California Trail ends here.

 **THE END**

You go around the toll bridge to save money. You'll have many river crossings and stops at forts to restock on food and ammunition—you'll need all the money you have. You plan to cross the Red Vermillion River farther up north, where it turns into a smaller creek.

The majority of your wagon train doesn't want to waste time taking that long route. They pay the toll and continue on ahead without you. Your smaller wagon train continues north alongside the river.

Bad luck strikes when you run into storms every day over the next week. The humidity won't break.

Sweat runs down your arms and legs. All of your animals are panting loudly.

When you finally ford the Red Vermillion River at a narrower point, your wagon train is irritable and wishing they'd just paid the toll. One afternoon, a hailstorm overwhelms your wagon. Your small wagon train drags along in the sweltering heat. There's no way you'll catch up with the families who paid the toll.

One afternoon, you and the McAllister children lie in the grasses of the plains, panting and exhausted.

"Will this end?" Fiona McAllister's freckled face is bright red, even underneath her bonnet.

"We're in a drought." Her brother Harry's face is shaded by book he holds up to block the sun.

You pull yourself up. "C'mon, let's go swimming."

"In the river?" Fiona's brow furrows. "The current looks a wee bit strong."

"We've got to cool down or we'll be in trouble." You reach out your hand and help Fiona stand up.

You lend a hand to Harry. "One minute. Just one more paragraph . . ."

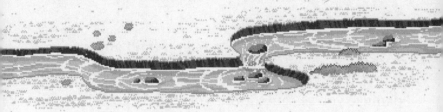

The three of you walk along the riverbanks and find a quiet pond nearby. Ducks are sitting along the banks. You're so excited to go swimming.

You dive right in, instantly cooled by the water. Fiona dips her legs in. Harry doesn't go near it. You shrug and duck your head under.

By suppertime, you're feeling very odd. You're hungrier than ever, but also nauseous at the same time. Maybe food will help calm your stomach. Should you eat now, or wait? ?

To eat, turn to page 38

To wait to eat, turn to page 81

You'll make it up to your wagon train any way you can. You won't have enough money to pay for all the damage you've caused, but you can try to barter and work off the rest.

Papa faces the crowd of angry scowls. "I'll help you fix whatever damage was done to your wagons."

"With what wood?" Fergus McAllister flicks his red mustache. "There's no tree in sight for miles, Keller. Ye can only do so much. Me wagon's got a damaged axle and two broken wheels, and I don't think that even ye can fix it all if I don't have the wood."

Mr. Southworth steps up. "I'll help too. It was an accident, and accidents happen."

"Accident!" Stella Beauregard raises her hands. "We could've lost half the wagon train to that stampede! Someone could've been killed!" She clutches her son George to her side. George sticks his tongue out at you. You pretend he is invisible.

"She's right." John Beauregard plants himself in

the middle of the crowd. "Accident or not, it was foolish and cost a lot of people. It's going to take more than your offering to help fix this, Keller. A lot more."

Some members grumble that you and your family should just leave.

Mama shakes her head. "Well, we can try to give you all some of what we have. But we don't have much, and we need every penny if we're going to get out West."

"You think it's any different for us?" John tilts his head. "It's going to take more than an apology and a few repairs to set this right."

You and your parents gather what little money you have in a small sack and place it on the ground in the center of the wagon corral.

"This won't be enough, we know." Papa's shoulders slump. "But it's all we have."

You've given everything you have to the rest of the wagon train. You don't have the supplies to continue on the trek West.

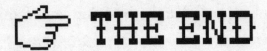 **THE END**

It's the hardest decision you've made thus far on your journey, but going to California is the right thing to do. Your mother hasn't seen her brother in years, and even without gold, California is filled with opportunities. Despite your family's concern over the drought and the long trek through the desert, you're prepared. It won't be easy, but you'll have the rest of your wagon train with you.

You choke back tears and hug Mr. Southworth goodbye. You've traveled so far together; you can't imagine going the rest of the way without him. But you've got to keep moving.

"We'll come to visit you once we get things all settled." Mr. Southworth squeezes your hand.

"Once you buy your freedom?"

He nods. "Exactly. I'll strike it rich either in the gold fields or with this little darling." He pats his fiddle case. "She's brought me luck so far."

"I hope so—and please say 'hi' to your mother. You'll keep in touch, right?"

"Promise." He winks.

You smile.

"We're going to miss you terribly." Mama puts her arm on Mr. Southworth.

"Likewise, Kutomá." Mr. Southworth smiles. "But we'll see you again. I know it."

At around ten o'clock, your smaller wagon train sets off on the California Trail. Mr. Southworth's wagon disappears over the hills.

Your trek takes you southwest by the majestic American Falls: enormous gushing waterfalls. You stop to stare in wonder. The falling water is rhythmic and soothing.

You travel through a thick stretch of sage into rockier territory and arrive at Goose Creek Valley. Mama collects some sagebrush to use in recipes and herbal medicines.

"It's especially good for your stomach." She pats her belly. "If you feel sick, or bloated, this will help."

Then you enter the famous Thousand Springs Valley, an oasis in the Great Basin filled with natural springs both hot and cold, and find temporary refuge

at Humboldt Wells, an area of marshy springs and small ponds of water.

You stay there for two days to fully stock up on water. Getting further into the Great Basin Desert will not be an easy feat. A summer storm passes through that night, soaking the springs and flooding the wells with fresh water. You and Benji run around in the rain with Fiona and Harry, knowing that it won't be like this in the desert. You feel refreshed.

The storm reinvigorates your weary wagon train

to push forward at a steady pace. As you make your way along the California Trail, the grass grows shorter and browner, disappearing into dry dirt and sand. The rolling green hills turn to rocky beige crags. Your only safety net is the Humboldt River, which you're following all throughout the Great Basin Desert.

The sun beats down hotter every day. Dry winds sweep up and begin to dry out your lips, causing them to crack.

Roughly ten miles from another set of hot springs, you come to a gaping canyon. The river runs directly through it.

"Carlin Canyon." John stretches out his arm. "There are several river crossings through this route."

Four river crossings would've been easy several days ago, but now the water is rushing through the canyon due to the recent storm. It's just your luck that you've been traveling this whole time in a drought, and now, in the middle of the desert, the river may be too high to cross.

"There might be another way, Cap'n." Fergus

McAllister approaches his wagon and points west. "A Bannock woman at Fort Hall told me that we could take an alternate route over those hills. It'll be about ten miles before we rejoin the Trail."

John dips his hand into the river and shakes his head. "I don't know 'bout that. Seems to me that we're going a bit far out of our way." He surveys the river. "It's not terribly deep. We'd have to caulk the wagons, but it could be done."

You're not so sure. Then again, going over hill country, away from the river, doesn't seem like a great idea either. What should you do?

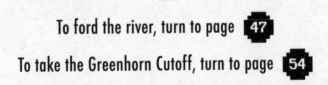

To ford the river, turn to page **47**

To take the Greenhorn Cutoff, turn to page **54**

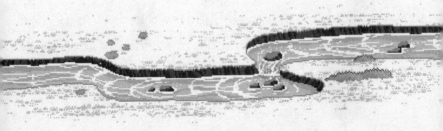

You should wait for the medicine to really settle in your stomach and avoid taking more. You put the medicine back in her bag and wait. You drink as much water as you can that night, and in the morning, you go down to the nearby Sweetwater River to collect more to boil over the fire. You're feeling a little better.

Mama notices you don't eat breakfast and brews you a cup of special tea she's brought from home—an herbal mix with ginger and lemon seed meant for indigestion. You drink it, but edge farther and farther away from the bacon in the skillet. The smell of food still makes you nauseous.

You walk over to Mr. Southworth and help milk his cow, Dilly. You then groom your horse, Spot, before the day's travel begins. You know you won't be eating any bad buffalo again.

Two days before you reach South Pass, you stop to make camp in a place called Rock Creek. Word spreads that gold was recently discovered in this area. Eager to try his own hand at mining, Mr. Southworth goes off with a pickax and panning tins to see what he can find. You follow him.

"Well, a small nugget, at least." Mr. Southworth smiles and wipes his brow on his sleeve. "A bit more trouble than it's worth, don't you think?"

You nod and plop down on the ground. Your sweaty legs stick to the grass. "I'll say."

Mr. Southworth picks up the nugget, sets his tools aside, and retrieves his fiddle from his wagon.

A merry tune trills out into the sunset hours, reviving weary spirits and cheering up those who haven't struck gold yet. By the time you and Mr. Southworth return to the wagon corral, his hat is overflowing with coins.

"I think you struck gold another way." You grin.

He laughs. "I think I did."

As you continue on through gentle winding hills,

thunder rumbles overhead. The sky opens up into a downpour, and the wagons go even slower. Your six oxen struggle against their yoke as lightning strikes down only yards away. Benji clutches Mama's arms as she controls the reins.

The next moment, you hear a *CRACK* and an angry groan. Your wagon grinds to a halt.

As the rain dies down, the wagon train stops. Folks huddle around your wagon. Mr. Southworth rushes over to help Papa inspect the wheels. They both shake their heads. It's not good.

"Broken wheel rim and axle, *and* dented iron tire." Mr. Southworth rubs his head. "Must've gone over a bad rock and banged it up pretty bad."

John Beauregard stomps over. "We need to press on if we want to make it through South Pass before day's end. Can you fix it?"

"Not that quickly." Pa sighs.

After debating with your family and other members of the wagon train, the rest of the wagon train elects to go on—without you. You'll have to fix your wagon and catch up to them. Even the McAllisters are moving on. Only Mr. Southworth offers to stay behind with you.

"Listen, Ben." He kneels down to tie his shoe. "I can help you fix this. This'll need more than a carpenter's hand, and I think you know it."

Papa wipes his brow. "You may be right, but I can't ask you to stay behind with us."

"I'm offering." He stands up and brushes off his pants. "That axle's going to need some tending to. Got the tools with me. We'll catch up with them in a few days, for sure. Besides, I can't leave you and your family out here alone. I know you'd say the same if I were in your position."

Papa nods with a heavy sigh as he turns to you. "What do you think we should do?"

You're not sure what to say. You know Mr. Southworth is right: Papa's going to have a hard time fixing the axle on his own. But you also don't want to separate Mr. Southworth from the rest of the wagon train. What should you do?

To accept Mr. Southworth's offer to stay,
turn to page **88**

To decline Mr. Southwourth's offer to stay,
turn to page **26**

You hurry to find your parents and secretly show them the small nugget you found embedded in the rocks near the ranch.

"Shiny!" Benji reaches for it. You quickly shush him, glancing around your wagon corral in the hopes that no one nearby heard him.

"We shouldn't keep this." Mama frowns. "You found this on the land of Rancho Johnson. This belongs to them, no matter how much we would like it."

You're disappointed, but you know she's right. The gold nugget is theirs, even if you did find it.

"But what if there's more nearby?" Papa puts his hand on Mama's shoulder. "Should we stay or keep going to Sacramento?"

You know the answer from the look on your mother's face. "We should keep going to Sacramento, Papa. We're almost there, and we might not find another nugget like this here, anyway."

Your family agrees that you'll keep moving on to your final destination of Sacramento. You're excited to see your three cousins you haven't seen in years.

You ask Harry and Fiona not to tell anyone about the gold nugget you found. You're afraid that the ranch might be robbed if word got out. They swear to keep the secret. You return the gold nugget to Mr. Johnson. He thanks you for your honesty and discretion.

"There's been talk of bandits hunting down pioneers who might be carrying gold." His mustache twitches. "I'm glad you haven't told anyone about this. I've heard some pioneers along the Carson Trail got robbed only a few days ago."

Now you're even more glad that you took the Beckwourth Trail. Though you hope it wasn't the other half of your wagon train that got robbed.

After resting overnight at the ranch, you and the others continue south to Sacramento. But the following night, you hear the sound of hoofbeats nearby, followed by quiet murmurs and a low laugh echoing across the landscape. You scramble out of your tent and strain to look out into the darkness. You hear several voices in the woods nearby, which grow fainter by the second. But you still hear bits of their conversation. It's the infamous River Rush Gang, who've been robbing pioneers all along the Oregon and California Trails. They're planning on attacking and robbing Rancho Johnson!

You sneak out to alert the night guard on duty.

The guard sounds the bugle. Startled, people bolt up out of their tents, bleary-eyed, including your parents. When you tell everyone what you heard, the wagon train isn't sure what to do.

"What can we do about it?" Fergus pounds his fist in his hand. "Go after them?"

You hurry over to your horse, Spot. "I can!" You're still in your pajamas, but you manage to get your boots on. "I'll beat them there and warn them."

"No." Mama's face screws up. "It's too dangerous. If those bandits catch you—"

"I'll be fine, Mama, I promise. You know I'm a faster rider alone than with you or Papa."

"I'll go." Papa looks at Mama. "It's the middle of the night."

"No, I'm smaller and faster. Let me do this. We've come this far, and I haven't let you down once. I'm ready for this." You turn Spot around sharply. "You know I'm right, Papa. We don't have time to debate. I'll be right back. But everyone at the ranch will be in trouble if we don't."

You make a stop by the night guard, ask for his bugle, and then dig your heels into the horse's sides, taking off into the woods. You stay off the beaten path and steer clear of the River Rush Gang; you see their torches in the distance. You get ahead of them and reach Rancho Johnson minutes before they do, sounding the bugle. William Johnson rushes out of the adobe house. It doesn't take long to explain the dire situation to him, and he readies his own defenses and assures you he'll be prepared.

In the end, Johnson and his staff ambush the bandits and tie them up to take them to the nearest sheriff in the morning. After Johnson thanks you profusely, you return to your wagon train. Your

Sacramento, CA
SEPTEMBER 5, 1851

parents are so relieved that they let you sleep for the next whole day inside the covered wagon. By the time you wake up, you've reached Sacramento!

Sacramento is warm, dry, and greener than you expected. Papa builds a new house on a plot of land with trees, with the Sacramento River nearby, and a bustling town that's perfect for Papa's carpentry business. Your uncle lives close by to your new house, running a general store with your aunt and three cousins around your age. It's been great to get to know them better, and you know that Fiona and Harry, who also live nearby, will get along with your cousins famously.

Papa works both as a carpenter and tries his hand at gold mining at several camps. Although you help him find several tiny nuggets, you and your family realize that the Gold Rush has been somewhat overhyped. Still, you don't regret making the move out West; in fact, the opposite. You're looking forward to not having to trudge through snow in the winter!

In the next few months, you receive a letter from

Mr. Southworth, and keep in regular contact with him afterward. Some time later, he writes to tell you that he's earned his and his mother's freedom—not by solely mining in the gold fields, but also by playing his fiddle! You're overjoyed. Not only that, but he's become the first African American man to serve in the Oregon militia. He comes to visit your family before heading back north to Eureka to play his fiddle in the gold camps there.

In the end, your journey has been long and arduous, but rewarding all the same. You can't be more excited for your new life in Sacramento. Congratulations! You've completed your journey on the Oregon–California Trail!

 **THE END**

GUIDE
to the Trail

THE OREGON–CALIFORNIA TRAIL

You are about to embark on a historic journey just like 400,000 pioneers who traveled between 1841 and 1870. You are headed west to seek your fortune during the Gold Rush. The trek is two thousand miles (3,220 kilometers) along the Oregon-California Trail. Everything you need is tightly packed into a covered wagon. Along the way you'll see majestic landscapes, meet new friends, and experience adventure and danger that will challenge you like never before.

GO WEST

Making the long and often dangerous trek will take all of your grit, smarts, and skill. You'll rely on your wagon train community as well. Keep on the lookout for bad weather, overflowing rivers, and bandits looking to rob pioneers along the Trail. Rest when you need to. Listen to your fellow pioneers, but trust your instincts. Don't take cutoffs unless you've done your research and know exactly where they lead. Stick to the Trail and stay well-stocked on food and water. Preparation is key.

Your days will start as early as four in the morning, with breakfast, chores, and loading your wagon. A seven a.m. bugle means it's time to start the long day's journey. The wagon train will roll along until six p.m., except for an hour's lunch and rest time, called "nooning."

At the end of the day in a corral, you unload your wagon, set up camp, take care of your livestock, and cook dinner. If you can't find firewood or kindling, you can burn dried patties of buffalo dung called "buffalo chips." Around the campfire you can tell stories, get to know your fellow pioneers, and listen to music.

PACK YOUR WAGON

Your ten-foot-long covered wagon will carry your supplies and the items you need for your new life. There won't be room to ride in the wagon, so you'll walk alongside it. Choose carefully, and pack only what is most important. Don't overload your wagon!

You will need two hundred pounds of food per person for the journey: mainly flour, bacon, sugar, cornmeal, fat, beans, rice, vinegar, baking soda, and citric acid.

Don't forget essential building, gold-mining, and wagon-repair tools, such as additional wagon wheels and axles. Caulk your wagon with tar when crossing rivers, and oil the wagon canvas to keep out the rain. You should also take camping gear such as a tent, bedding, kitchen utensils, matches, and candles, as well as useful things such as rope, a rifle for hunting wild game, animal traps, and a medicinal kit.

Avoid the temptation to take luxury items, such as fancy foods, heavy furniture, or dressy clothes. Finally, it's important to buy a team of six slow but sturdy oxen to pull your wagon.

Spend your money wisely. You don't want to use it all before you get to your destination of either California or Oregon. Sometimes you might need to pay for repairs or for more food. Buy only the bare minimum when needed. You don't want to reach your new life completely broke!

JOIN A WAGON TRAIN

Pioneers will band together into wagon trains, which are groups of wagons traveling together. Smaller groups are more manageable, but if you're traveling with a larger group, be sure to keep everyone together at all costs. The advantages of larger wagon trains include safety in numbers, helping each other with skills, and hunting together. There are many dangers on the Trail, so a larger wagon train will likely mean better chances of survival and success.

It is the wagon train captain's job to decide when the wagons start in the morning, when they finish at night, and when to stop for lunch. The captain also assigns guards and decides what order the wagons travel in. No one wants to always travel at the end, breathing in the dust from the other wagons, so you will all take turns.

MEET REAL PIONEERS

You just might meet these real-life pioneers on the Trail.

JAMES [JIM] BECKWOURTH
[1798–1866 OR 1867]

James, or Jim, Beckwourth was an African American pioneer, explorer, trail guide, fur trapper, rancher, and mountain man. Known for fantastic and illustrative tales of his time in the West, Jim Beckwourth had his life story published in *The Life and Adventures of James P. Beckwourth: Mountaineer, Scout and Pioneer, and Chief of the Crow Nation* (1856).

The son of his owner and an enslaved woman, Jim Beckwourth was freed by his master. Making his fortune as a wrangler and fur trapper, he claimed to have been adopted by the chief of the Crow Nation. He married the chief's daughter and remained with the tribe for several years.

In 1851, he led a group of pioneers along a former Indigenous trail.

Named the Beckwourth Trail, this alternate route boasted a low incline and smoother roadways than the well-known Carson Route. It led to Marysville, a town that renamed their largest park after him more than a hundred years later in the 1990s. Beckwourth died in Denver, Colorado Territory—present-day Denver, Colorado—at sixty-seven or sixty-eight years old. The exact year of his passing is unknown.

JOHN BIDWELL
[1819–1900]

John Bidwell was an American pioneer whose family came from England during the Colonial era. He was a soldier, gold miner, U.S. congressman, and was most famous for helping lead the first organized wagon train of the Bidwell-Bartleson party from Missouri to California.

In 1841, he and a portion of the wagon train split off for California as opposed to continuing on the well-known Oregon Trail. With only vague directions, he led everyone across the Great Basin Desert into California, where he settled at Sutter's Fort in Sacramento and became very successful during the Gold Rush. From his purchase of Rancho Chico, he eventually founded the city of Chico, California.

He was known to work alongside the Indigenous people in the area and treat them with respect rather than hostility, as many others did during the fever of the Gold Rush. His wife, Annie, also held deep moral convictions, and was a fierce advocate for Indigenous rights, as well as being a suffragette. Although he put in an unsuccessful bid for president, he and his wife remained well-known figures in the community and longtime friends to the Indigenous tribes in the area.

LOUIS A. SOUTHWORTH
[1829–1917]

Louis Southworth was an African American pioneer, soldier, gold miner,

In the collection of the Benton County Historical Society Museum

and fiddler who bought his freedom by playing the fiddle in gold-mining camps across Oregon and California. He was born to Louis and Pauline Hunter, who were enslaved by James Southworth, and traveled with his mother and Southworth to Missouri when he was four years old.

In 1851, he and his mother continued on with Southworth along the Oregon Trail to Oregon, where Louis tried mining for gold to earn his freedom. Instead, he found that by playing fiddle in the gold mining camps, he made much more money. He traveled down to Northern California and finally earned his freedom with his fiddle.

After eventually returning back to Oregon, he got married to a woman named Maria Cooper, adopted a West African child named Alvin McCleary, and became the first African American man to join the Oregon militia. He settled down in Corvallis, Oregon, to become a farmer and beloved member of the Corvallis community. He passed away at eighty-six years old, a famous pioneer and Oregon legend.

DANGERS!

DEHYDRATION

On the Oregon-California Trail, crossing the desert presents great dangers of dehydration, even if you're near water. Make sure to stock up on clean water, to drink as often as possible, and watch for signs of dehydration: nausea, dizziness, and severe headache. Try to keep out of the sun, if possible. Travel at night, if necessary.

DIFFICULT TERRAIN

Along the Oregon and California Trails you'll encounter some of the most challenging terrain in all of the United States. You'll have to ford rivers, cross the over seemingly endless desert sands of the Great Basin, make your way through desert river canyons, and much, much more. Be sure to be adequately prepared with enough food and water. Hunt when you can, and always stop for water when you find it.

BAD WEATHER

You will be passing through all different climates on the Oregon-California Trail. Sudden thunderstorms, hail, and traversing through the desert can damage wagons, destroy food and livestock, and result in sickness and death if you're not properly prepared. Keep additional wagon wheels and axles on hand for repair. Stay well-stocked on food and water and ration carefully.

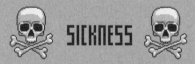

SICKNESS

Cholera and dysentery are deadly diseases on the Trail that can kill a person within a day. Highly contagious and contracted by drinking unclean water or eating uncooked food, cholera was the main cause of death on the Trail. Symptoms are shaking, fever, diarrhea, and vomiting, and usually death. Cook your food thoroughly and boil drinking water—or drink coffee, which will boil your water anyway.

DISHONEST PEOPLE

The Trail is riddled with bandits and people wanting to take advantage of pioneers who are headed out for the Gold Rush. Be sure to listen to those trusted people around you, stay on your guard both day and night, and remain cautious along the Trail.

CROSSING RIVERS

Crossing rivers can be difficult for heavy wagons filled with supplies. While expensive, sometimes paying to cross a ferry or a toll bridge might save your wagon train from being destroyed by a river that's too dangerous. Make sure the river is low if you're going to ford it, and have tar buckets on hand to caulk the wagon cracks.

☞ FINDING YOUR WAY

In 1851, once you leave Independence, Missouri, you are striking out into the open wilderness of the Great Plains and southwest desert terrain. There are very few settlements along the way, with no roads or towns. The United States comprises thirty-one states and busy cities and towns back East, but out West, you'll have to cross territories and Indigenous lands by using a map of the Trail and looking for famous landmarks listed here in the Guide to the Trail.

Ask for help and advice whenever you can. At settlements and forts along the way, often trail guides and friendly locals can provide good advice, especially if there are unknown dangers or bad weather up ahead.

Look for these landmarks between Missouri and Oregon City

DISTANCE FROM INDEPENDENCE, MISSOURI:

FORT LARAMIE: 650 miles (1,046 km)

FORT HALL: 1,217 miles (1,959 km)

SACRAMENTO, CALIFORNIA: 1,720 miles (2,768 km)

OREGON CITY, OREGON: 2,000 miles (3,220 km)

BIBLIOGRAPHY

Baldwin, Peggy. "Louis Southworth (1829–1917)." The
    Oregon Encyclopedia, last modified March 17, 2018.
    oregonencyclopedia.org/articles/southworth_louis_1829
    _1917_/#.W5fLiehKiUl.

"Beckwourth Trail." Trails West, accessed September 10, 2018.
    emigranttrailswest.org/virtual-tour/under-construction.

"Jim Beckworth." Encyclopaedia Britannica, accessed September 10,
    2018. www.britannica.com/biography/Jim-Beckwourth.

"James Pierson Beckwourth: African American Mountain Man, Fur
    Trader, Explorer." Colorado Virtual Library, accessed September
    10, 2018. www.coloradovirtuallibrary.org/digital-colorado
    /colorado-histories/beginnings/james-pierson-beckwourth
    -african-american-mountain-man-fur-trader-explorer.

"John & Annie." Bidwell Mansion State Historic Park, accessed
    September 10, 2018. http://bidwellmansionpark.com/history/
    john-annie.

"John Bidwell." Oregon–California Trails Association, accessed September 10, 2018. www.octa-trails.org/emigrant-profiles/john-bidwell.

"Louis (Lewis) Alexander Southworth." Oregon Secretary of State, accessed September 10, 2018. sos.oregon.gov/archives/exhibits/black-history/Pages/families/southworth.aspx.

"Louis Southworth, an Oregon pioneer." African American Registry, accessed September 10, 2018. aaregistry.org/story/louis-southworth-an-oregon-pioneer.

Williams, Vivian T. "Lou Southworth, Pioneer Oregon Fiddler." *Old-Time Herald,* accessed September 10, 2018. www.oldtimeherald.org/archive/back_issues/volume-11/11-1/southworth.html.

The Oregon Trail™

LIVE the Adventure!

Do you have what it takes to make it all the way to Oregon City?

Look straight into the face of danger and dysentery.

Read all the books in this new choose-your-own-trail series!

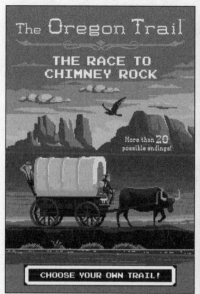

The Oregon Trail

THE RACE TO CHIMNEY ROCK

More than 20 possible endings!

CHOOSE YOUR OWN TRAIL!

The Oregon Trail

DANGER AT THE HAUNTED GATE

More than 20 possible endings!

CHOOSE YOUR OWN TRAIL!

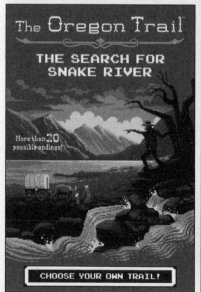

The Oregon Trail

THE SEARCH FOR SNAKE RIVER

More than 20 possible endings!

CHOOSE YOUR OWN TRAIL!

The Oregon Trail

THE ROAD TO OREGON CITY

More than 20 possible endings!

CHOOSE YOUR OWN TRAIL!

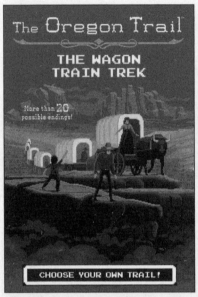

The Oregon Trail

THE WAGON TRAIN TREK

More than 20 possible endings!

CHOOSE YOUR OWN TRAIL!

The Oregon Trail

ALONE IN THE WILD

More than 20 possible endings!

CHOOSE YOUR OWN TRAIL!

The Oregon Trail

GOLD RUSH!

More than 20 possible endings!

CHOOSE YOUR OWN TRAIL!

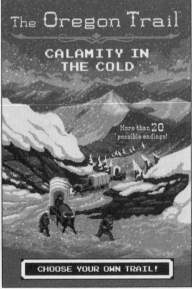

The Oregon Trail

CALAMITY IN THE COLD

More than 20 possible endings!

CHOOSE YOUR OWN TRAIL!